the Dress Designer's Promise

Wedding Bliss, Book 2

USA TODAY BESTSELLING AUTHOR

MELISSA McCLONE

The Dress Designer's Promise
Wedding Bliss (Book 2)
Copyright © 2024 Melissa McClone
Second Edition

Original version published as *SOS Marry Me!*.

Cover by Alt 19 Creative

Cardinal
PRESS

Cardinal Press, LLC
January 2024
ISBN-13: 978-1-944777-80-7

DEDICATION

For my own Belles: Shirley Jump, Myrna Mackenzie, Linda Goodnight, Susan Meier, and Melissa James. Talented authors and amazing friends!

Special thanks to: Missoula County Detective David Brenner, Idaho County Sheriff Larry Dasenbrock, Virendra Gauthier, John Frieh, Virginia Kantra, Michael Leming, Dru Ann Love, Mike Mooney, Anne Ryan, Tiffany Talbott, and last, but not least, Carol Hennessey, Jen Hensiek, and Le Ann Martin with the Clearwater National Forest.

1 take full responsibility for any mistakes and/or discrepancies.

PROLOGUE

March

On the final day of her girls' weekend in Lake Tahoe, Serena James stood in the lobby of the gorgeous Starr Lake Inn, which looked like it belonged in the Swiss Alps, not Nevada. She and her two friends were staying with Kelsey Addison in her lovely Victorian home nearby.

So far, they'd thrown the newlywed Kelsey a belated bridal shower and a bachelorette party. Those should have happened in February, but her wedding happened with such short notice none of them could attend. It was only March, so they weren't that late. This was the first time all four of them could be in the same place. They'd also eaten an incredible variety of food, especially at the inn's brunch this morning. Serena was glad she wore leggings today because she doubted she could zip her pants.

Everything about the long weekend had been

wonderful, but the best part was spending time with Kelsey, Jane Dawson, and Elle Cavendish. The four of them met as college freshmen during sorority recruitment and were thrilled to discover they would be in the same sorority's pledge class on bid day. That was over eight years ago, and they'd stayed friends even though they lived in different states now. Thanks to the wonders of technology, their group chat kept them in daily contact.

The warmth from the crackling fireplace made Serena want to curl up in one of the chairs and sink into a book with a cup of spiced tea before she flew home to Boston that afternoon. But Kelsey seemed to have other ideas. Given the itinerary Kelsey, a wedding planner, had handed them when they arrived on Wednesday, that didn't surprise Serena. Thank goodness Elle had asked Kelsey to reserve two time slots before she arrived. They'd used those to surprise Kelsey, who might've had an idea of what they were planning, but she didn't let on at all.

Serena grinned. "I don't remember anything other than brunch on our schedule this morning."

"Me either," Elle agreed.

Jane nodded. "So what are we still doing here at the inn?"

"Are we going on a walk?" Living in Boston, Serena wasn't used to spending much time outdoors in nature unless she took a walk through a park, and she'd enjoyed the snowshoeing yesterday. The fresh mountain air refreshed her tired soul.

"Or doing a craft?" Excitement filled Elle's voice. She was the ultimate DIYer of the group. Jane did her fair share of crafting too, though cooking was more her passion.

Jane tilted her head. "Maybe Kelsey needs our help with an upcoming wedding. It wouldn't be the first time we stuffed invitations into envelopes or tied ribbons on favors."

That was true. They had all helped Kelsey launch her wedding planning business right after graduation. They still helped each other out as much as they could from a distance, like when Serena had sent Kelsey a vintage veil and headpiece she'd found in Paris. Kelsey had ended up wearing it when she married Will on Valentine's Day. Speaking of which...

"Wait." Serena glanced around. "Where did Kelsey go?"

"You guys. I'm up here." Kelsey stood at the staircase railing, her complexion glowing. If not for the mimosas they all drank during brunch, Serena would've thought her friend was pregnant, given how radiant she appeared. "We are doing exactly what Elle suggested in our group chat before I got married."

Elle's nose crinkled. "I don't remember saying anything."

Kelsey held a bouquet of white flowers in front of her. Not just any bouquet—a bridal bouquet made of ranunculus and roses and tied with a white satin ribbon. "It's time for the bouquet toss, and one of you is going to catch it."

Serena clapped. Maybe this would be the impetus Rupert needed to finally propose. They'd dated long enough to know they were meant to be together. "Fun!"

"You only think that because you have a boyfriend," Jane mumbled.

"Exactly." Elle stepped back. "I was joking when I texted that. I forgot to turn on my sarcasm font."

"Were you really joking?" Kelsey teased, holding up the flowers. "Because I caught the bouquet at my cousin Christina's wedding, and look what happened to me."

I want that to happen to me. Serena positioned herself front and center. "I'm ready."

"Take your positions," Kelsey announced.

"You don't have to toss a bouquet," Elle said. "You already did that on your wedding day."

Jane nodded. "Didn't you say Faith caught that one?"

"She did, but she'll never get married. At least not anytime soon. So this is a do-over with my three closest friends." Kelsey's smile reached all the way to her eyes. Love and marriage suited her. She gently waved the beautiful flowers. "And since none of you were at the wedding, this is the perfect time for it."

"We were there in spirit," Jane said.

"That's right," Elle agreed.

"Yes, you were." Kelsey grinned. "And now you're all here in person, so we're doing this."

"I was just caught up in the moment. I mean, a Valentine's wedding is so romantic, but…" Elle stepped back and pointed at Jane and Serena. "Please aim in the direction of one of them. I don't plan on getting married. Ever."

Elle's fiancé had cheated on her right before their wedding day, and now she wanted nothing to do with men. Serena didn't blame her friend for feeling that way. Elle's life had imploded in the worst possible way, and they'd done what they could to pick up the pieces and help her.

"I don't mind catching the bouquet," Serena offered.

Elle crossed her arms over her chest. "It's yours. Unless Jane wants a shot."

"Nope. Between working at the coffee shop and starting the catering business, I don't have time for romance. Aim for Serena, please." Jane stepped to the side. "She and Rupert can be the next to get married."

Serena wiggled her toes. Marriage hadn't come up directly in conversation, but they were aligned on their future. All he had to do was buy a ring and get down on one knee.

So why wouldn't he propose?

They'd dated long enough and were the perfect couple. Even Mom and Dad approved of him, which was saying something because they barely approved of Serena. No matter what she did or the success she had as a wedding dress designer, it wasn't quite good enough for them. Yet she kept trying to make them proud of her.

"It has to be fair," Kelsey announced. "I want everyone to come to the center."

Jane trudged over next to Serena. With a frown on her face, Elle inched that way slowly as if wading through wet concrete.

"On three." Kelsey turned around so she couldn't see them. "One, two, three…"

The bouquet flew over her shoulder, arcing toward the three of them. It was headed straight toward Elle.

No way.

Their friend had been through too much with her cheating fiancé. If Elle caught the bouquet, she'd put on a brave face and then cry once she was alone.

Serena, however, was ready to get married and be as happy as Kelsey and Will were together. Catching the bouquet would not only protect Elle, but give Serena what she wanted so badly—a husband and a family, one where she was accepted and loved unconditionally.

She'd never been athletic but would give it her all right now for Elle's sake and her own. Serena jumped higher than she'd ever jumped in her life and snagged the flowers midair. "It's mine!"

She clutched the satin-covered stems. As the floral

scent wafted in the air, she brought the flowers closer and inhaled. Now, Rupert wouldn't have an excuse. He would have to propose.

Her life plan was one step closer to being realized. She couldn't wait.

CHAPTER ONE

November

Though Serena's heart pounded in her chest, she attempted to appear nonchalant. She stood in the lobby of the elegant brownstone that housed her design studio and the other wedding businesses renting space from Belle Mackenzie, an event planner known as the Wedding Belle, who'd moved to Boston, where her late husband was from. "I'll go to the bridal show."

"Well, darlin'," Belle purred in her distinct Southern drawl. If anything, her accent had gotten stronger over the years, or maybe that was just Belle's style. "That's sweet of you to offer. We do need some positive publicity after the fiasco of the Vandiver wedding cancellation. None of us should have been blamed the way we were, and the bridal show's sponsors would be delighted to have one of the country's up-and-coming wedding dress designers fill in at the last moment."

Serena caught a glimpse of herself in a gilt-framed mirror. At least she looked normal, so no one would know what a mess she was inside. She took a steadying breath and quickly glanced at Rebecca, a wedding photographer, and Calista, a florist. The others renting were busy with appointments and couldn't join them in the lobby.

"I've always wanted to visit Seattle, and the Pacific Northwest must be lovely in the fall." This would work. Serena kept her smile firmly in place. "The Vandiver cancellation was unfortunate, but at least you aren't dealing with another one of Faith Starr's wedding cancellations."

"That's true." Belle tilted her head. She was a beautiful woman with coiffed silver hair and a generous, glossed smile, and she gave the best hugs this side of the Mason-Dixon Line. "Though I feel for what your friend Kelsey must have gone through in February after the fifth one."

Serena nodded. "At least Kelsey used the wedding she'd planned to marry Faith's brother, so the cancellation worked out this time."

"Yes, it did." Belle hesitated. "I appreciate you offering to go to Seattle, but you usually avoid bridal shows, and you were already out west this spring when you had that girls' weekend in Lake Tahoe. I can't imagine you want to travel across the country a second time this year."

"I'm sure about going." Serena hoped she sounded

willing but not desperate to get out of town again. "Besides, there really isn't anyone else who can attend."

Belle drummed her French-manicured nails on the glass table in the lobby filled with ivory and bridal-pink furnishings. "That's true. We all seem to have an extra serving or two on our plates these days."

"Well, whoever goes to Seattle"—Calista brushed a lock of dark-blond hair off her face—"I want them to take my wedding gown to the show."

Serena shook her head. "No way."

"You're getting married in just a few weeks," Belle said a beat later.

"On the twenty-second to be exact, but we need to show brides that the Wedding Belle and the rest of us offer the most premier wedding services in the world," Calista explained. "That means showing off what we do best—everything from Nadia's delicious cakes to Serena's stunning designs. Serena's entire line is beautiful, but my custom gown is her latest and most exquisite creation."

"But it's your wedding dress." The thought of flying cross-country with the gown made Serena's stomach churn. "I made it to fit you, not some size-zero model. And I wouldn't want to risk getting makeup or runway stains on the silk."

"That doesn't mean you can't display the gown on a mannequin in the booth."

Serena imagined everything that could go wrong with that scenario. She shook her head emphatically this time. "What if something happens to the dress while it's on display?"

"Nothing will happen to it." Calista winked across the table. "Not if you're the one who goes to Seattle."

Serena appreciated her friend's vote of confidence and wouldn't let Calista down. "If this is what you really want, I promise to take care of your dress."

Belle rubbed her chin. "Charlie offered to have his son fly whoever goes, so nothing will have to be checked with an airline."

Charlie was the man Belle was currently seeing. Dating seemed a better adjective, but Belle was adamant they were only friends. None of them believed that, but they humored her. Charlie was younger than her and appeared quite smitten, bringing her lunch a few times a week.

Calista leaned toward her. "Oh, wait. Did you and Rupert have plans for that weekend?"

Serena gritted her teeth at the mention of her boyfriend's—make that ex-boyfriend's—name, but her smile remained steadfast. She'd kept the news of their breakup a secret in light of Calista's upcoming wedding. She didn't want to be a downer when everyone was looking forward to their friend's nuptials. "Rupert's been traveling a lot himself. He won't mind."

At all.

He'd dumped her two months ago, but she hadn't told anyone. Not even Kelsey, Jane, and Elle. Serena kept telling herself it was because she didn't want to dampen her friends' spirits given how well everything was going for them. Kelsey was so in love and married to her dream guy. And Serena didn't want to cast a dark shadow and be the brokenhearted friend with Calista's upcoming wedding events. But the real reason was simpler. Serena still hadn't figured out what to say because she was so embarrassed.

Until the breakup, her life had been working out according to plan. She had a successful dress design studio, a lovely condo, and a Roth IRA. The next step had been to get married. She'd thought she had found the right guy, but she was too focused on the result to realize he hadn't been so right.

"It's fine if I go to Seattle," she added for herself mainly, but if it convinced the others, then all the better.

"You've got yourself a good man, Serena," Belle said. "After Calista, I'm sure there'll be another wedding to plan. And I know exactly what cake you'll want Nadia to bake for you and Rupert. Chocolate with orange-flavored-fudge filling."

"And I know the flowers." Calista's green eyes twinkled like the mini fairy lights she used with yards of tulle and garlands of blossoms. "White dendrobium orchids, green roses, green cymbidium orchids, and white and green parrot tulips."

White and green. One of Serena's favorite color combinations. Calista knew her tastes so well.

A cake. Flowers. Serena's colleagues had her

perfect wedding figured out. The only thing missing…
was a groom.

A weight pressed down on the center of her chest.
She thought of the nearly completed wedding dress
hanging in her hall closet. Okay, she'd been foolish and
tempted fate by starting on the gown before she had a
ring on her finger.

But who could blame her?

Her relationship with Rupert Collier had
proceeded right on schedule. They had dated for nearly
two years, met and liked each other's families, and
talked about the future and starting a family, which was
what Serena wanted most of all. Becoming engaged
was the next obvious step.

She'd started working on her wedding dress
because she'd wanted time to get every stitch and detail
exactly right. She'd chosen the fabrics and design using
the same care with which she'd chosen Rupert Collier.
Not only was he smart, gorgeous, and rich, but he was
also ideal husband and father material. Everything
she'd been looking for in a man, everything her friends
expected her boyfriend to be, and everything her
parents wanted her to marry—he had it all.

Until, impatient for a ring after dating exclusively
for so long, she'd shown him the bouquet, moved past
the vague talk about their future, and brought up the
M-word.

Marriage.

Rupert had complimented the floral design and

said they would discuss marriage later. He hadn't stuttered or balked at the word. She thought nothing was wrong. So when their second anniversary approached two months ago, she broached the topic again.

Suddenly, her perfect boyfriend wasn't ready for a serious relationship. He accused her of being too selfish and too self-reliant to make a permanent commitment.

Oh, he'd wanted to keep seeing her, she remembered bitterly. They looked good together, and his boss liked her. But he'd wanted to take a serious step backward in the commitment department. He'd even suggested they date other people.

As if…

Serena had said no, thinking he wasn't serious about being nonexclusive and trying to see if she was serious about their relationship, but Rupert had said goodbye. Proving once again that, if she didn't do what others wanted, she wouldn't get what she wanted.

His parting words had stung.

"You don't need me, Serena. You don't need anyone."

Over the past two months, she'd realized he was right. They were better off without each other. She didn't need him. She hadn't loved him the way a woman should love the man she wanted to marry. He looked great on paper, but she hadn't loved him as much as she liked how he'd fit into her plans.

So much for her perfect dress. Her perfect groom. Her perfect life.

She forced herself to breathe. A setback? Yes. A total failure? No. Serena James didn't fail.

Rebecca grinned as if she'd found the perfect Kodak moment to capture with her camera. "Rupert hasn't been around much. He'll have to adjust his travel schedule once you get married."

Serena's stomach roiled. Her temples throbbed. She hated keeping secrets from these women, women who were more than coworkers. She had to find the right time to tell them—tell everyone—the truth.

Serena hadn't wanted her bad news to affect everyone else's joy. She hadn't wanted her breakup to take anything away from any of the newly engaged or married couples' happiness. And as the days turned into weeks, she still couldn't find the right time to tell everyone she'd been dumped.

It wasn't only the happy couples. Elle still wasn't over being cheated on and dumped. Nadia, a single mom, was down on men, too. Telling them the truth would only reaffirm their belief that Mr. Right didn't exist. Serena couldn't do that to them. They'd already faced too much disappointment and heartache.

Besides, her friends expected more from her.

Everyone did.

Serena worked hard on her polished image, kept a positive attitude, and was always there in a pinch. People counted on her. They looked to her as someone who could do anything. She wasn't the kind of person to fail, not in life or in love. That wasn't an option. Her friends expected her to find Mr. Right. The same as Serena expected of herself.

Which was why she would find someone to give her the perfect love, family, and life she dreamed about. Just because she'd been wrong about one man didn't mean her one true love wasn't out there somewhere. Maybe even in Seattle.

"So about the bridal show…" Serena leaned back in her chair. "What else do I need to bring besides the wedding dresses?"

GROUP CHAT #1

Serena's suitcase was packed. She just had one more thing to do. Something she'd been putting off. She typed on her cell phone.

Serena: *Hey, I just wanted to let you know I'll be in Seattle until Sunday. Belle needs someone at the big bridal show, and I'm it.*

Kelsey: *Rupert must be traveling. No way would he want you out west again without him.*

Serena: *It's not like this is a pleasure trip. I'll be working like crazy.*

Jane: *I love Seattle. I wish I could take the train up there and see you, but I know you'll be busy.*

Elle: *Don't you have an event to cater this weekend?*

Jane: *There's that too.*

Kelsey: *Take lots of pics, especially of any new trends.*

Serena: *I'll report back on everything. Promise.*

Chapter Two

Kane Wiley ducked around the business jet's engine to place his bags in the plane's exterior storage compartment. His breath steamed in the November air.

"Is that all you've got?" Dad asked.

"Yep." Not only for this flight. All Kane owned—besides the plane itself—could fit into two bags. He traveled light and liked it that way.

"I appreciate your making the trip, son." Wearing faded jeans, a black turtleneck, and a down vest, Charlie Wiley looked younger than his fifty-six years, even with his salt-and-pepper hair.

"Just hold up your end of the deal, Dad."

"I will." Dad picked up a cooler containing soda, water, ice, boxed lunches, and a plate of cookies and brownies that would go into the galley. "I'll leave you alone. No more questions. No more badgering you to come home."

Home.

That was a good one. Kane nearly laughed.

There hadn't been a real home to come back to since Mom died suddenly from a heart attack three years ago and his dad had quickly remarried and divorced. Now, his father looked poised to make the same mistake again with another woman.

"But..." Charlie pushed the cooler through the doorway of the cabin. "I still expect a card or text or phone call at Christmastime."

"I can manage that." Easter and Father's Day, too. Even his dad's birthday.

Kane would do anything to get away from Boston and never return. He didn't want to watch his father woo and wed yet another woman who could never take the place of his mother.

"Just remember, I love you, son." Dad's voice cracked. He took a breath. "I'm here if you need me. For anything. Money, whatever."

Kane nodded once, then glanced at his watch. "Where is she?"

"Belle?" Dad asked.

Kane fought the urge not to wince at Dad's newest *friend*'s name. "The one I'm flying to Seattle."

"Serena will be here. Traffic is always bad at this time."

Norwood Memorial Airport was twenty-five miles north of Boston. That meant she could be really late. Kane bit back a sigh of frustration. He wanted to get in the air sooner rather than later.

"Try smiling," Dad said. "You might have fun. Serena James is a beautiful young woman."

"There are lots of beautiful women in the world. No need to settle on just one."

Though a cross-country romance might not be too bad. As long as it was over by the time they returned to Boston.

Dad shook his head. "You just haven't met the right woman to love yet."

"I meet lots of women," Kane said in a matter-of-fact tone. "Love them, too."

Dad frowned. "I meant the forever kind of love. The kind I had with your mother."

And with his second wife.

And with what's-her-name. Belle.

Forever was a joke. And love—the kind Dad was talking about—was nothing more than a pretty word for companionship.

A white van pulled through the gate and honked its horn.

Dad turned toward the sound. "They're here."

"Great." Kane had been hoping they would be a no-show.

A woman with silvery-blond hair and a beaming smile drove. She waved. Her passenger held a cell phone to her ear and wore round, dark sunglasses that hid much of her face.

The van stopped, and the driver's door opened. The older woman, wearing brown pants and a colorful jacket, slid out gracefully.

"Good morning." She greeted Dad with a smile and a hug. The woman stepped toward Kane, extending her arm. "You must be Kane."

He shook her hand, noting her warmth and strong grip. She was different from his mother and his ex-stepmother. Older. Maybe even older than his father. That surprised Kane. "You must be Belle."

"I am." Her voice sounded like honey. Slow and sweet like Deep South honey. "I appreciate you flying Serena to Seattle."

Of course she did, especially with his father paying the associated flight and fuel costs.

"Kane's happy to do it," Dad answered without missing a beat. "Aren't you, son?"

Kane nodded. He would be happy once this trip was behind him so he could fly away for good.

"Well, we'd better get busy, then." Belle opened the van doors and pulled out a box. "We have boxes to load. Brochures, favor samples, and portfolios. Plus linens, flower arrangements, a frozen cake, and gowns."

Belle's eagerness to help surprised Kane. "O-kay."

"You still have to meet Serena James. She's a talented wedding dress designer," Belle said. "She's finishing up a phone call. I'm sure she's letting Rupert know she's at the airport."

Kane bit. "Rupert?"

"Her boyfriend." Belle's ever-present smile widened. "The two are practically engaged. By New

Year's, I'm guessing she'll be wearing a diamond on her left ring finger."

So much for a little romance in Seattle. Ring on the finger or not, Kane didn't mess around with another man's girl.

The passenger door opened. He focused on the woman exiting the van.

She was, in a word, stunning. Long blond bangs fell over her forehead, and her hair flowed down the back of her jacket. The style looked hip and trendy, just like the woman herself.

She wasn't tall, five-six if he was generous and subtracted the heels on her brown leather boots. Even with her long wool coat, he could tell she had curves in all the right places.

He liked what he saw. She was exactly his type.

Kane blew out a puff of breath that hung in the cold air. Old type, he corrected with a frown. He'd given up on blondes.

Her hair color and how she dressed reminded him of Amber Wallersby, a former girlfriend. She'd wanted him to stop flying his grandfather around on the private jet and take a boring desk job at one of her father's companies so he could pamper her in the manner she was accustomed to. Kane had almost agreed and been taken in until he'd seen that she might have been gorgeous on the outside but was all show and had zero substance on the inside.

Was Serena James the same?

Not that he was in any position to find out. Or care. Still, they would be spending several hours flying west together. No sense starting off on the wrong foot.

"Hi," he said. "I'm your pilot, Kane Wiley."

Serena didn't extend her hand. She removed her sunglasses and glanced up at him. Clear, sharp eyes met his. He hadn't expected such directness or such stunning blue eyes.

"You're Charlie's son?" Serena sounded surprised, almost as if she disapproved.

"In the flesh."

"Do you see a family resemblance?" Dad asked.

She glanced back and forth between the two men. "Not really."

"Oh, I do," Belle said. "Like father, like son. Both of you are quite handsome."

Dad beamed.

Kane rocked back onto his heels. He wasn't anything like his father. He didn't need a woman in his life—not on a permanent basis, anyway. And unlike his father, Kane's loyalty was hard to earn and his disapproval slow to fade.

"The eyes are the same," Serena conceded. "Maybe the chins, too."

The way she studied him made Kane uncomfortable. "We're running late. Let's get your stuff on board."

Serena glanced at Belle.

"Is something wrong, darlin'?" the woman asked. "Did you get a chance to call Rupert and say goodbye?"

"Um, no."

A pink flush deepened the color of Serena's cheeks.

Interesting. Kane wouldn't have thought her the blushing type. She seemed too cool and collected, but maybe leaving her "practically fiancé" had rattled her.

"Would you mind if the gowns went in the cabin, Mr. Wiley?" she asked.

"It's Kane, and no, I don't mind."

The relief in her eyes was almost palpable. "I'll put them in the cabin."

"I'll load them."

"I don't mind doing it," she said.

"That's okay. I'd rather do it myself."

Serena eyed him warily. He waited for her to challenge him and was surprised when she didn't.

"You can put the food in the galley if you want," he offered. "It's in a cooler near the door."

"Fine."

Not fine if the tightness around her mouth was anything to go by. At least she didn't pout like Amber. He removed several long, bulky white dress bags from the van.

"Kane prefers doing things his own way," Dad explained loudly enough for Kane to hear.

"So does Serena," Belle added. "She likes being in control."

"Then the two of them should get along fine."

Nope. The exact opposite.

Flying with two captains in the cockpit was a recipe for disaster because neither wanted to give up control. And that meant one thing. It would be a long flight to Seattle and back.

* * *

Serena had a checklist for her Mr. Right: polite, attentive, articulate, and smartly tailored. All qualities her parents had taught her to value. All qualities Rupert had possessed in spades.

All qualities Kane Wiley lacked. She couldn't afford to be attracted to him.

Maybe she could pivot and date Kane if he were more like Rupert. That might be easier to explain than being dumped. But unfortunately, he wasn't close to being her Mr. Right. He was more like a bad boy, reminding her a little of her ex-brother-in-law, and she would not follow in her sister's footsteps.

No way.

Serena moved to where he'd secured the gowns and checked each of the dress bags. She repositioned three of them. Not much, but she felt better taking control. That is, taking care of her dresses. That was her job, even if Kane didn't seem to realize that.

The dresses were her responsibility, no one else's, and the man was arrogant and rude for not letting Serena take care of them herself. He seemed to be the opposite of his kind and generous father, who epitomized a true gentleman. If not for the price of the flight—free, thanks to Charlie—and the ability to personally oversee the transport of the gowns, Serena would have found another way to Seattle. But they couldn't afford to be too choosy after being blamed for and losing money on the Vandiver cancellation.

She thought about how much Kelsey and Will were in love. Calista and her fiancé, too. Serena would find the same kind of forever love they had found. All she needed was her Mr. Right. A man who not only looked good on paper, but whom she could also love.

Glancing out of a window, she caught a glimpse of Kane as he performed his preflight walk-around. Light glinted off sun-streaked light-brown hair that fell past the collar of his dark leather jacket. A jacket that emphasized his broad shoulders.

Talk about Mr. Wrong.

Some women might have found him good-looking. If they liked tall, classically handsome guys with chiseled jawlines, square chins, sharp noses, and intense brown eyes.

Serena didn't object to any of those things, exactly. She just preferred them packaged in a suit and tie and paired with a short, styled haircut and clean-shaven face. She didn't want a man who looked like he'd rolled out of bed, bypassed the razor, and raked his fingers through his hair as an afterthought.

He glanced at the plane—at the window she stared out of, to be exact—and his gaze met hers. His eyes, the same color as her favorite dark chocolate, made her heart bump.

Uh-oh.

She hurried back to her seat and sank into the comfortable leather club chair. The temperature in the cabin seemed to rise even though the door was still open. She removed her coat, picked up her sketch pad, and fanned herself.

What was the matter with her? Of course, she hadn't been sleeping well lately. Or eating, either. One good meal and she'd feel better.

She'd like to take a bite out of Kane.

"Hot?" a male voice asked.

Her sketch pad fell onto her lap, and she looked up.

Kane stood at the entrance of the plane. The interior suddenly seemed smaller. He appeared larger.

She gulped. "Excuse me?"

"Are you hot?"

"I—I…" Something about him made her flustered and tongue-tied and heated. She didn't like those feelings, either. "I'm a little warm."

"I'll take care of it." He closed and latched the door. "Are the wedding dresses okay?"

Serena heard the challenge in his voice and raised her chin. "They're fine. Now."

The intensity in his dark eyes sent heat rushing through her veins. She sucked in a breath and looked away.

"Seat belt fastened?" he asked.

Not trusting her voice, she grabbed the straps and fumbled with the buckle until it clicked into place.

"The same rules apply on this flight as a commercial flight," Kane explained. "When we reach cruising altitude, you can visit the lavatory or help yourself to anything in the galley."

"No flight attendant?"

"Not unless you want to fly the plane while I serve you lunch and a beverage." He pointed out the exits and where the oxygen masks were located. "If we lose cabin pressure, place the mask over your nose and mouth and breathe normally. Did you bring a laptop?"

"No." She'd wanted to escape from the constant pretending of her life in Boston. Her prying friends, fake phone calls, and even emails were a hassle these days. "Just my cell phone. I know not to use it during the flight."

"Even if you miss your boyfriend?"

She tried not to cringe, but the thought of lying to a total stranger left a bitter taste in her mouth. "It won't be a problem."

"Not using your cell phone or missing him?"

"Either."

At least that was the truth.

"If you need anything," Kane said, "let me know."

Serena could just imagine his reaction if she asked for, oh, a bag of pretzels and a fiancé. She bit back a smile.

No matter how desperately she wanted to maintain her image and be the daughter her parents expected her to be, she would never ask someone like Kane—someone so obviously wrong for a woman like her—to help her find a new Mr. Right and one true love.

She could do that on her own. And would.

Rupert was right. She didn't need anyone and could do everything herself.

CHAPTER THREE

"The doors will open in ten minutes," a feminine voice announced over the loudspeakers in the convention center.

Ten minutes? Kane scanned the large hall, balancing the gold-wrapped box he'd promised to deliver to Serena. He thought he'd had more time.

Little Miss I'm-in-Charge Serena had sounded upset when she'd called and asked if the box was still on the plane. When Kane had finally found the package in the tail cone baggage compartment and brought it over, she told him she'd be right out. But he was there, and she wasn't. Somehow, that didn't surprise him.

Not that he was upset to run this errand for her, because he was curious to see her in action. Interested enough to volunteer to deliver the box himself.

But man... He shivered. Kane was sorry now. All the white and pink and lacy wedding stuff gave him the heebie-jeebies.

He might as well have been standing in the middle

of a nightmare—wedding-themed, of course. Instead of fire, heat, screams, and pipe organ music from some cheesy Dracula movie, this place reeked of flowers, tulle, fairy lights, and an orchestral soundtrack.

A woman dressed in black with spiked red hair, flushed cheeks, and a clipboard in her hand raced up to him. "Are you a model for the fashion show?"

"No."

"Where could they be?" Her face scrunched, then brightened as she studied him. "Would you want to be one of the models?"

Kane pictured himself dressed like a penguin, escorting models in white dresses down a runway. He didn't mind models, but the other stuff? Not his thing. "No, thanks."

With a frustrated sigh, she ran down the aisle and disappeared out of sight.

She wasn't the only one in a hurry. Exhibitors rushed around, putting finishing touches on their booths themselves, straightening tablecloths, and applying lipstick. Kane didn't see many men—not like yesterday when he'd dropped off Serena to set up. He wondered if they were doing errands or something. Not to sound sexist, but this seemed like the last place any guy like him would choose to spend an hour. Let alone a day. Or two.

At one time, he'd considered settling down someday, but now, after all he'd seen, Kane knew better. It was best to remain single so he could do what he wanted, not forced to be someone he wasn't.

As he searched the booths, every company seemed to have the word *wedding* somewhere in its name, and the similar colors and vibe made everything indistinguishable. Talk about overwhelming. He might as well have been in Neverland or Narnia. That's how lost and out of place he felt.

"Kane."

He turned toward the sound of his name and saw Serena waving at him.

"Over here," she added.

Relieved to find Serena, he walked across the aisle to her booth. Whatever panic he'd heard in her voice when she'd called him earlier wasn't visible on her face, which appeared fresh and rested with expertly applied makeup.

That's right, dummy. Look at the lipstick. Keep your eyes on her face. She's so not your type anymore.

But man, she looked attractive in that dress.

Her gaze was intent on him. "You made it."

"With minutes to spare."

"Minutes?"

"A few. Getting worried?"

Kane knew that the answer was yes. She seemed to keep a tight hold on her responsibilities and pretty much everything within her influence. It was probably a good thing she had an almost-fiancé. With the way she looked, he could have been tempted into something casual with her, but the last thing he wanted or needed in his life was a cool blond control freak with a thing for weddings.

Serena took the box from him. "I wasn't worried, but I was getting a little impatient."

"Not the patient type?"

"Waiting for someone to come through can be hard."

"Sometimes."

He wouldn't mind waiting at her booth. He didn't have to want to spend the rest of his life with her to enjoy the view before him. What man with blood running through his veins wouldn't want to look at Serena?

She defined the "it" girl in every possible way. Her brown-and-blue dress clung in all the right places. The hem fell above the knee, and her high heels made her legs look long and sexy.

He didn't know whether to envy that Rupert fellow or pity him. Serena James was the type who knew how to make a guy roll over and beg. And Kane didn't sit, stay, or play dead for any woman, no matter how hot she looked in heels.

"I do appreciate you bringing this over." She walked toward a linen-covered table with one of the elaborate floral arrangements she'd brought with her in the center. Candles in silver holders sat on either side. She tossed a smile his way. "Thank you."

Her gratitude sounded genuine. Kane couldn't tell whether she was sincere, but he was willing to play nice. "You're welcome."

The gentle sway of her hips and the graze of her

dress hem above her knees captured his attention again. The lingering scent of her light floral perfume tickled his nose.

Serena opened the box. "Now all I have to do is set out these things, and the display will be ready."

The table looked finished and fancy enough to him. A little too fancy for his taste, but probably what the monkey-suit, bouquet-tossing crowd expected. "What's in there?"

"Chocolate." As she unwrapped each item, she placed the pieces of candy on an oval beveled-edge mirror sitting on the table: three chocolate truffles shaped like three-tiered wedding cakes; small gold and silver boxes tied with ribbon; oval- and heart-shaped engraved chocolates packaged in a gold box and wrapped with tulle and a ribbon; and engraved gold- and silver-foiled coins. "No wedding is complete without something chocolate."

"I don't care much for weddings, but I like chocolate."

Her eyebrows rose at his not-so-subtle hint, but she tossed a coin his way.

He unwrapped the gold foil and took a bite. Good stuff. High end. "Aren't you having any?"

"I don't sample the merchandise," she said in her cool, controlled voice.

Yeah. Right. Probably one of those salad-and-rice-cake types who wouldn't let herself eat a piece of candy. Too bad. She had a curvy figure, but he'd rather see a woman enjoy a meal with dessert than starve themselves.

She walked over to a round table displaying a white four-tiered wedding cake and lifted the linen tablecloth to hide the box underneath. When she stood, she straightened one of the real flowers cascading from the top of the cake like a colorful pink-and-white waterfall. "All done."

He'd say so. Judging by this booth, Belle's wedding business was a high-class, high-end operation. He shouldn't have been surprised based on what Dad had said about her, but their booth was a step up from the sea of pink and white. From the neatly stacked full-color brochures to the warmth of the maroon embossed-leather photo albums, everything exuded "luxury" and "wealth," including Serena herself.

Kane leisurely finished his chocolate as he surveyed the booth. He noticed a stack of boxes. Board games, actually. Who would have thought to make a game out of getting married? Playing that sounded more like torture than fun.

A burgundy upholstered chaise lounge sat at a right angle to a row of headless mannequins dressed in white—the Wedding Shop of Horrors. "Looks like someone went furniture shopping last night."

"We worked with a rental store here in Seattle who delivered all this yesterday."

"You must have worked all night."

She pushed a strand of hair back from her face. "Just doing my job."

"I thought you designed wedding dresses."

"Each of us helps out where we can," she said. "That's why working with Belle is so fun."

Fun? Serena never seemed to stop working. At least not in the short time he'd known her.

She moved through the booth, adjusting swags of rich yellow fabric draped on the boring white panels separating each of the exhibit areas.

Did she ever slow down or rest? Even on the flight, she'd worked on something. He didn't know how she did it.

"Everything looks good," he said.

"Good won't cut it. Brides are the pickiest people on this planet, next to their mothers." She straightened a stack of brochures. "Everything needs to be perfect."

"Nothing's ever perfect."

"Then you've never attended a wedding put on by Belle." Kneeling, Serena realigned the hem of one of the wedding dresses. "Or worn one of my gowns."

"No offense, but I don't look my best in a train and heels."

She smiled up at him.

He smiled back.

Something passed between them—the hum of attraction.

Now, this was more like it.

"Do you need anything?" he asked. "Breakfast? Coffee?"

Me?

A weekend romance in Seattle wouldn't have sucked. He wouldn't be sticking around Boston after he dropped her off, so he never planned on seeing her again.

"Thanks, but I already ate, and my coffee is stashed where I can reach it easily." Standing, she peeked at her watch. "You might want to leave. The doors are going to—"

"Welcome to the Northwest Fall Bridal Extravaganza!" the voice over the loudspeaker announced.

"Uh-oh. You didn't make it out in time. Watch out." Serena smoothed the skirt of her dress. "We're about to be overrun by the bridal brigade, commanded by mothers and supported by best friends, sisters, and cousins."

Within seconds, chattering, laughter, and even shrieks filled the large hall as if someone had turned off the mute switch on the remote. Packs of women stampeded past him. Some wore heels, and he had to admit that their speed was impressive and a tad frightening.

"Where are they going?" he asked.

"The first fashion show."

Had he agreed to model, all those women would have been running to him. Wonder what Blondie would have said to that. A smile tugged on his lips.

Two young women approached her with questions about the cake on display.

Women lugging ten-pound bags of bridal literature now crowded the once empty aisles and booths. Lots of women. Young ones, old ones…mostly young ones. Good-looking, too.

And engaged.

He didn't do engaged women. Or even almost engaged women like Serena.

"Mom." A twentysomething woman with chestnut hair, wearing a green babydoll dress, rushed into Serena's booth. "This is it. I must have this dress."

"We've been here two minutes, and that's the third dress you've said that about," the mother said.

"Mo-om."

Serena was speaking to two other women, but that didn't stop the mother from interrupting the conversation.

"How much is this wedding gown?" the mother asked.

"I'm sorry, but that dress is not for sale," Serena calmly explained with a smile. "It'll be worn at a wedding in a few weeks."

The daughter's filler-injected, shimmery pink lips puckered like a bizarre human-hybrid fish. Kane grinned to himself. Maybe this was the Northwest version of a bridezilla.

"Could you make one like this for my daughter?" The mother flagrantly showed off her designer purse and iceberg-size diamond rings.

Despite the interruptions, Serena smiled pleasantly.

"I can create a dress just as beautiful for her. With your daughter's lovely figure, an asymmetrical A-line gown would be stunning. A cutaway skirt, even. And champagne embroidered lace would be a wonderful accent with her coloring."

The bride tossed her artfully streaked hair. "We'd pay you extra for that dress on display."

Kane would have told the mother to take her money and… Well, go someplace else.

"If you're interested in our gowns, we have a few samples here that can be sold off the rack." Serena's smile never wavered as she motioned to the photo albums on the table. "You might also want to make yourself comfortable and glance through our portfolio to get a taste of our designs."

"We might come back later." The mother looked down her surgically designed pert nose. "Or not."

The words didn't seem to faze Serena. "I'll be here."

She handled herself well against the woman's appearances-are-everything, I-can-buy-whatever-I-want attitude, and that impressed Kane. He only hoped she wasn't cut from the same cloth.

Not that it meant anything to him if she were.

As the bride stomped away, more women fawned over Serena's dresses. When she answered their questions, she not only promoted her gowns, but also the services provided by everyone who worked in Belle's building.

Serena was in her element—glowing, sparkling, and radiant.

Kane slowly backed away. As much as he enjoyed watching her, this was no place for a single guy intent on remaining that way.

Serena gave a quick nod his way. He was surprised she'd observed him leaving. He was also surprised he liked her noticing.

Uh-oh. Not good. Very bad, actually.

Serena James might not have had a ring on her finger, but avoiding her was the smart thing to do. The right thing to do, even if he spent another night in his hotel room by himself, watching TV. On second thought, maybe he could find a bridesmaid sprinkled among the brides and their mothers with something on her mind besides marriage, then find a bar or a club to visit.

Maybe all the shiny fabrics and chocolate would put her in the mood for a casual night out. And maybe that would get his mind off a certain "practically engaged" someone.

As he glanced back at Serena, his chest tightened.

Or…maybe not.

* * *

Part of being at a bridal show was networking, and that was what Serena had done tonight at a cocktail party after the event. She'd planned on taking a shower and crawling into bed after that, but a friend from a design program invited her to dinner, just the two of them, and she hadn't the heart to say no. They were friends, good friends, but he'd turned on the charm as usual, and she'd appreciated the attention. But now that they were back in the hotel lobby, she was ready to call it a night.

"Thanks for taking me out to dinner, Malcolm. The food was delicious and the company better." Serena kissed Malcolm Rapier's cheek, expertly avoiding the last-minute turn of his head in an attempt to meet her mouth. She shouldn't have been surprised given the way he'd flirted with her over the years. She'd thought that had been a game to him, but now, she wasn't so certain. "It's been great catching up with you."

"Sure you don't want to go to the party?" With his boyish grin, he looked more like one of his models than the rising star of men's formalwear design. "I'd love to show you off."

Serena was tempted. He'd always been a looker, and in a stylish black suit he'd designed himself and a multicolored silk tie, he was almost as handsome as Kane.

Where had that come from?

"I usually enjoy being shown off, but I didn't sleep much last night." Going out wasn't a good idea when all she wanted to do was yawn. Not to mention, her feet ached from standing all day.

"Understood. Return of the bridezillas tomorrow." He laced his fingers with hers. His hands were warm and smooth like the fabrics he dealt with every day. "But if you change your mind, call me and I'll send the limo back for you." He'd gone all out for their dinner tonight with their transportation to the restaurant.

"You're too sweet."

Unlike her pilot. *The* pilot, she corrected.

"No, you're too beautiful and look great on my arm." Malcolm twirled her to him as if they were dancing and pulled her against him. "Any chance you'd leave Boston for Seattle?"

Serena knew exactly how the game was played.

Normally, she would concede, but not tonight. She didn't like the way Kane kept intruding on her thoughts. She wanted to prove to herself that the pilot had no effect on her by playing along with her friend a bit.

She stared at Malcolm through her eyelashes. "Why would I want to do that?"

"Oh, Serena, my muse, can't you imagine the beautiful formalwear we could create together? Paris, Milan, New York. Nothing could compete with us."

"You're right about that." But Serena wanted more than that kind of partnership. She dreamed of finding true love—marriage and children. She eyed Malcolm subjectively as if taking inventory of the pieces for her next design. "Would this be strictly a business arrangement?"

42

He lowered his mouth to her ear, his warm breath tickling her skin. "Do you think I'd ask you to relocate across the country just for a job?"

Maybe she was taking things too far. Okay, she and Malcolm would make a stunning pair. They shared common interests and enjoyed each other's company. Yet if she were at all interested in pursuing a relationship with him, why couldn't she get Kane out of her mind?

His smile widened. "You're thinking about it."

Not really. At least not with him. She shrugged.

"You are." Laughing, Malcolm caressed her cheek with his fingertip and kissed her forehead. "Until tomorrow, my soon-to-be Seattle love and partner."

With that, he walked out of the revolving door to hit tonight's trendy parties. Truth be told, she wasn't sad to see him go.

Serena's heels clicked on the marble floor of the hotel lobby. She wasn't as lively as earlier, given that her body's internal clock was running three hours ahead, but she had no complaints about the show.

The first day of the Northwest Fall Bridal Extravaganza had been a hit, an "in-the-park home run" to quote one of the Seattle show's organizers. Tomorrow might be a grand slam, given that Serena already felt like an all-star.

"What would Rupert say?"

Serena recognized the voice and stopped. She was annoyed that Kane was not only on her mind, but now

43

there. He was sitting at a nearby table with a pint of beer, looking comfortable and at ease. In his jeans and black long-sleeved T-shirt, he had that sexy, carefree, I-don't-care-what-you-think style down. Not that she thought he was sexy. Her type of sexy, that was.

Oh, she'd once been tempted by bad boys, but Morgan's experience had made Serena immune to their charms. Her sister had fallen in love with a guy who had women calling him day and night. He had no steady job nor a desire to acquire one. Morgan had moved in with him anyway and then married him, claiming he loved her and would change.

He hadn't, and he didn't.

Serena had been the one to pick up the pieces when her brother-in-law's infidelity destroyed their marriage and left her pregnant sister devastated and alone. Their parents still hadn't forgiven Morgan for falling in love with the wrong man and "ruining" her life. Not even the birth of Brayden had made a difference.

"What do you mean by that?" Serena asked.

Kane motioned to an empty seat.

She really shouldn't, even if a part of her really wanted to.

He pushed the chair out from under the small, round table with his foot. "You can buy me a drink for this morning."

Her mouth curved. "You already have one."

"I wouldn't mind another."

She did owe him for dropping off the box on time,

even if he had waited until the last possible minute. She sat, grateful the moment her bottom hit the leather chair and she was no longer standing.

"Oooh," she moaned.

His eyebrows lifted. "You're easily satisfied."

She flushed. "I should look into designing a high heel that can be worn for fourteen hours straight without causing foot pain."

"I meant the guy. For a woman who's practically engaged, you seemed chummy with Mr. Suit."

Each time Serena heard that phrase—*practically engaged*—she felt as if another heavy bolt of fabric had been stapled to her shoulders. And right now, she didn't like Kane's judgmental tone. He didn't know her. He knew nothing about her.

"Are you a pilot or a chaperone?" she asked, removing one of her shoes.

"Pilot. Unattached. But if you were mine"—his gaze traveled over her with lazy appreciation—"I sure wouldn't want you having dinner or cozying up to another man."

Tingles shot through her, and she sat straighter. Her reaction had everything to do with being tired and nothing to do with him. "Then it's a good thing I'm not yours, isn't it?"

"A very good thing."

Serena winced. She wasn't used to such rudeness or honesty and didn't know what to say. That left her more than a little flustered. She could always be counted on to find the right words or do the right thing.

"Let me guess," he continued. "Your boyfriend is a carbon copy of the guy you were with."

"Malcolm Rapier is the guy's name, and he's a little like Rupert." Only better. Malcolm dressed much better than her ex. "He's a fellow designer and a friend."

"Who wants to be more than a friend."

It wasn't a question. "And you know this because…"

"I'm a guy."

Serena wiggled her toes. "And guys know everything."

"You said it." Kane raised his glass.

"Malcolm likes pretty things."

Kane took a swig of beer. "Things?"

"Women." She didn't know why she was wasting her time explaining things to Kane. "Malcolm likes to be seen escorting attractive women around. You know, arm candy."

Which was probably why he wanted her to move to Seattle. A built-in plus-one to take to social functions. Not exactly the strongest foundation for a lasting relationship.

Kane's mouth quirked. "Modest, aren't we?"

"You asked."

"I did." A beat passed. "So Rupert—"

"Doesn't worry." The words tumbled from her

lips. Not exactly a lie. Her ex-boyfriend didn't care what she did. "There's no need."

"You're a one-man woman."

"Yes, I am." When she had a man. "I've never understood people who play the field."

"As long as the individuals involved know what's going on, I don't see a problem with it."

She rubbed the arch of her foot on the bar of the chair. Man, she wished she could wear flats tomorrow. "That's because you're a guy."

"Women play the field, too," Kane said. "Otherwise, it would get mighty lonely out there."

"Have you been lonely tonight?"

"No." He swirled his glass. "I had dinner with a lovely bridesmaid who had only one thing on her mind."

Serena kicked off her other shoe. "What was that?"

"Becoming a bride."

Serena laughed. "You don't want to get married?"

"Nope," he said. "Marital bliss isn't for me."

She wasn't surprised. He didn't look like husband material. But if a woman were looking for a temporary boyfriend instead of something more permanent...

"What *do* you want?" Serena asked, curious.

He got a faraway look in his eyes. "Freedom."

She'd never known freedom in her entire life. She always worked toward something—fulfilling an obligation or meeting a responsibility. "I'm sure that must be nice."

"You should try it sometime."

Temptation sparked. And then she thought about her parents. She couldn't do anything to upset them. After their meltdown over Morgan's marriage and subsequent divorce, they'd pinned all their hopes and dreams on Serena's shoulders. They'd made it clear that if she disappointed them like her sister had by becoming a single mother, they would disown all of them, including little Brayden. Serena couldn't let that happen, but sometimes the weight of their expectations made it hard for her to stand straight.

She stared down her nose. "Not my style."

"Mr. Suit is your style?" Kane asked.

"Pretty much."

"Too bad."

"Not for Mr. Suit."

He nodded, then stopped. "Except for Rupert."

Serena rubbed both feet against the bar between the chair legs. It wasn't the best massage, but it was better than nothing. "Ah, yes. Rupert."

"Women like you need to open your eyes," Kane said. "The perfect guy could be right in front of you, but if he isn't your 'style,' you'll walk right by and miss your chance."

"Love will find a way."

Kane studied her. "You really buy into all this wedding stuff, don't you?"

"Completely," she said, wondering if she'd be able to put her shoes back on or if her feet had swollen already. Still, rubbing her arches had helped, so she'd figure it out when the time came.

"Well, then." He raised his glass to her. "I'm sure you'll find exactly what you're looking for."

"You, too. A juicy piece of eye candy like yourself must have women falling at your feet."

A smile erupted across Kane's face. The effect was devastatingly charming. Serena moistened her lips, trying not to stare.

"Juicy, huh? Thanks." He placed his empty glass on the table. "It's not often I get a compliment from an esteemed piece of arm candy."

"It's not often I give them." *Uh-oh.* She was flirting. But she kind of liked how it felt. "Do you want that drink now?"

"I'll take a rain check."

A twinge of disappointment ran through her. *Ridiculous.*

Serena was only having a little fun. Nothing more. She knew what she wanted to find, and it sure wasn't Kane Wiley.

GROUP CHAT #2

The following morning, when Serena opened her eyes, the hotel room was dark and cold. She'd turned down the heat last night, so this was the result. The blackout drapes were closed, but her body told her it was already morning. She was still on East Coast time, and she'd woken before her alarm. Good. That would give her time to pack, call the bellhop to grab her luggage, and snag a cup of coffee before heading to the convention center.

Serena glanced at her cell phone on the nightstand. Not quite six. She had plenty of time. She also checked her text notifications. Her friends had been chatty last night.

Serena: *I shared a Northwest Bridal Show album with you. Let me know if you want a closer look at anything, and I'll see what I can do.*

Kelsey: *Oh, I love all the photos. My brain is bursting with ideas.*

Serena: *Yours usually is, but I thought you might like some of the new spring trends.*

Kelsey: *Always!*

Elle: *How did your event go, Jane?*

Jane: *Great. I met the Posh Planner, a lovely woman named Rachael Reese, who's married to one of the billionaires of Silicon Forest. She asked for my card and said she would love to do an event together.*

Kelsey: *That would be amazing!*

Jane: *I hope she's serious.*

Elle: *Of course she is. Your food is amazing, and your skills are wasted at the coffee shop.*

Jane: *My job there pays the bills, but I got some ideas from Serena's photos, so I'll be experimenting in the kitchen today.*

Elle: *I'll leave the wedding stuff to you all.*

Serena: *Just woke up. Long day yesterday, but, Elle, you really need to make that wedding budget spreadsheet and planner you used into a product. Something like that would have gone over big here. Just sayin'.*

Jane: *That would be awesome.*

Kelsey: *Yes, it would, as I believe all of us have mentioned before, and I'm happy to provide funding.*

Elle: *Thanks, but I'm not ready to do something like that.*

Kelsey: *One of these days.*

Jane: *For sure.*

Serena: *And we'll all be here to support you when you're ready, Elle.*

Serena only hoped Elle could get past being cheated on by her fiancé and having to cancel her wedding. That heartache held their friend back in so many ways. Maybe Serena should at least tell Elle she'd been dumped. That might help her to know she wasn't alone.

Serena could think about that on the long flight home.

CHAPTER FOUR

The bridal show had ended a couple hours ago. Now, Kane eyed the altocumulus clouds to the west. No immediate danger there. The weather service had issued an icing advisory at high altitudes, but they'd be flying below the problem. His plane was only certified to forty-five thousand feet. Still, he was eager to get in the air.

As soon as his passenger got off her ridiculous pink cell phone.

"Yes, Belle," Serena said. "Both the local paper and the magazine took photos."

"Hang up," Kane ordered. "Time to go."

Serena held up a single, slim finger in response.

He'd already given up more than a minute.

Back at the convention center, photographers had swarmed her elegant booth, snapping pictures and jotting down quotes from Serena. It seemed she was a hotshot in the wedding world.

Kane had suffered the commotion as well and as

long as he could. He could see that success was important to her. Besides, his dad was paying for his time, so complaining would only get him a headache.

But after The Suit had shown up, eager to shower Serena with congratulations and kisses and who knew what else, Kane's patience had evaporated. He wasn't a clocks-and-schedules kind of guy, but the weather system pushing down from Canada wasn't waiting while Serena played kissy face with her designer buddy.

Now, Kane was waiting again. The plane had been fueled. He had loaded their food and luggage, filed his flight plan, and completed his walk-around. It was time—past time—to go. "Get in the plane."

She raised her index finger again, like a dog trainer warning a barking pooch.

Kane bit back a growl and grabbed her phone. "She's got to go," he said into the tiny receiver. "She'll call you later." He switched off the phone and tossed it into the plane and onto her seat.

"What did you do that for?" Lines creased Serena's forehead. "I was only on the phone for a couple of minutes."

"Try twenty," he corrected.

Serena opened her mouth but then pressed her lips together. She entered the plane. He followed her.

"A couple of storms are brewing with a low-pressure system off the Pacific." Kane locked the door. "The weather in Canada is moving south."

"Why didn't you tell me?" she asked in a huff.

"I tried. You were on the phone."

Serena removed her coat and took her iPad out of her bag. She picked up her phone, moved it out of the way, then sat down.

Kane recognized the silent treatment, especially the way her eyes avoided his. Amber used to do that. So did a lot of other women. He wouldn't let Serena make him feel guilty. Not when *she* should have been apologizing to *him*.

"The weather shouldn't affect us, but I don't want to take any chances. That's why I want to take off—to try to beat the storm coming in," he said. "So keep your seat belt fastened in case we hit any turbulence."

She buckled up. "Not a problem."

"Food's in the galley, but be quick about it because of the—"

"Turbulence." She finished for him. "I will. And, Kane…"

"Yeah."

"I'm sorry for taking so long." Her gaze captured his, her big, blue eyes apologetic. Appealing. Not like Amber at all. Not like any of the other women in his life. "I kept us from leaving the convention center on time, too, and I really appreciate you waiting for me. I was excited. I wanted to share the news of all the good publicity and photo ops with my friends."

He grunted. "No worries."

Kane lied.

He was worried plenty. Not about the weather

because he was a good pilot. Surface wind speeds were acceptably low, and the system coming in was moving slowly enough that it shouldn't be a problem.

His reaction to her, however, was a whole other story.

* * *

Serena stared out the small window at the overcast sky. Kane was upset with her.

Even though he'd accepted her apology, she could tell he didn't like being made to wait. She didn't like waiting, either. Time to make it up to him?

Not necessary, a voice in her head whispered.

He'd been a jerk.

He'd grabbed her phone.

He'd hung up on Belle.

Kane had explained all that. She could forgive his impatience to get in the air. She wasn't quite as ready to let go of his brusque rejection last night.

"Then it's a good thing I'm not your girl, isn't it?"

"A very good thing."

Serena bit her lip. Kane hadn't even let her buy him the beer. He'd wanted a "rain check."

Not that she cared. Not much, anyway.

Unless his wanting a "rain check" was his way of seeing her in Boston. Maybe it was time to find out.

They hadn't hit any turbulence. Now that they were at cruising altitude, Serena unfastened her seat belt and went to the galley, which reminded her more of a refreshment center than an actual kitchen. Still, the efficiently designed space made it easy to pour a cup of coffee, find two freshly baked cookies, and put them on a napkin. She carried everything to the cockpit.

Payback? Or peace offering?

Either way, she didn't want to owe Kane anything.

"I brought you a snack," she said.

He glanced over his shoulder. "What?"

"Coffee and chocolate chip cookies." He liked chocolate, she remembered. "I, um, owe you a drink, remember? There wasn't any cream—"

"Black is fine." He took the food from her. "Thanks."

Okay, she was done now. "I'll see you when we land."

"Come on in," he said at the same time.

Kane motioned to the other seat. "Sit up here for a while."

Serena stared at the high-tech instrument panel with a small computer-like device between the two pilot seats. Not a lot of space up here.

She glanced at the cabin. It was safer back there.

"Plenty of room," Kane said. "This baby's simple enough for one pilot, but it can be flown by two."

"I can't fly."

His attractive mouth curved. "But you can sit, right?"

She crawled into the seat and peered out of the

window. The one-hundred-eighty-degree view took her breath away. Clouds blanketed the sky as far as she could see. She couldn't tell where the ground was or where the sky ended. Forget about finding the horizon. "Wow."

The word described how she felt. Every nerve ending tingled. Her insides buzzed.

Being up here, cocooned in the small cockpit with Kane and cut off from the earth below, made all her problems seem a world away. A world she suddenly wasn't in any hurry to return to.

"Fasten your seat belt," he said.

The harness-style seat belt went over her shoulders and around her waist. When she had trouble buckling it, Kane reached over to help her. The warm skin of his hands brushed hers, sending tiny shocks all the way to the tips of her fingers.

Nothing. It meant nothing. "I've got it."

"Sure?" he asked.

She wasn't sure about anything. But she nodded and somehow managed to get the buckle clipped despite her trembling fingers.

"Most of the weather is behind us," he said. "It should be smooth flying. We might even make up some time."

"Good."

But it wasn't. Not really.

Serena wasn't ready to return to Boston. She wanted this time with no lies, no expectations to uphold, and no responsibility to last a little longer. The incredible views of Kane in her peripheral vision and the open sky in front of her didn't hurt. The bridal show in Seattle had been a success but also incredibly stressful. Coming off that high, then literally flying, she'd never felt such freedom as she did now.

Was that what Kane liked? The freedom? The ability to go wherever he wanted, whenever he wanted? She could understand the appeal now.

She glanced his way. "So...do you like to fly?"

He gave her a look.

Okay, dumb question.

Serena would try again. "How long have you been flying?"

"Since I was sixteen. It's the only thing I've ever wanted to do."

"Why did you choose to be a charter pilot and not an airline pilot?"

"I thought about doing the corporate gig, but it's too much like working for a bus company. My grandfather bought a business jet. When he offered me a job as his personal pilot, I jumped at it. I flew for him for six years until he got sick." Kane's mouth tightened. "He doesn't travel anymore."

Her chest tightened. "I'm sorry."

"Why? I got my hands on this plane for next to nothing, and my grandfather's instructions were to make my own way in the wild blue yonder. That's what I've been doing."

Serena envied his go-where-the-wind-carried-him attitude. She'd planned out her entire life. Rarely did she even go out to eat without reservations.

"How often do you fly?" she asked, wanting to learn more about him. Something about Kane Wiley intrigued her in a way she'd never felt.

"All the time." He patted the yoke. "This baby isn't only how I make my living. It's where I call home."

"Home." She thought about her painstakingly professionally decorated condo in Boston. "You and me. We're very different."

"Nothing wrong with that."

Serena nodded.

He was rootless, a wanderer. Free. She was tied down by her business, responsibility, and expectations.

But at this moment, for as long as it could last, Serena wanted to enjoy the flight and this time with Kane, both despite their differences and because of them. She wanted a taste—a nibble, really—of what his life was like.

"You're such a free spirit," she said.

"I like to go where I want to go."

"And Boston?"

"A layover," he said. "Nothing more."

"Isn't your family there?"

"My dad." Kane pushed a couple of buttons. "We don't always see eye to eye on things."

"My sister is like that with my mom and dad. That's made things…difficult." For all of them.

"What about you and your parents?" he asked.

"I get along fine with my folks." She'd made sure of that.

"Lucky."

Serena nodded. But feeling lucky had nothing to do with her parents and everything to do with the sexy man sitting next to her. She held back a sigh.

A button lit up on the instrument panel. Kane immediately noticed it. As he straightened in his seat, his brow furrowed.

Her heart jolted. "Is something wrong?"

"Nope, but I need to take care of that light." He studied the instrument panel. "Would you mind going back to the cabin and fastening your seat belt?"

"Sure." She unbuckled the harness and squeezed out of the seat. "I'll see you later."

He nodded, pulling out a manual.

Serena returned to her seat and buckled her seat belt. Leaning back, she blew out a puff of air.

What had she been thinking? Worse yet, what had she been doing up there?

That warning light had been a sign, a reminder that she was better off earthbound. She needed to get her head out of the clouds. Being up in the air was a dangerous place. And being with Kane...

She didn't want any turbulence in her well-planned life. Morgan and Brayden depended on her. She couldn't afford to veer from what Mother and Father wanted for her or it would negatively affect her sister and nephew.

* * *

Why was engine number two's fuel filter light on?

Kane focused on the instrument panel. He reset the circuit. The light remained on.

Interesting.

He had dealt with this before and knew what to do, but with Serena on board, he glanced at the flight procedure's manual to make sure he hadn't forgotten anything.

Okay. Just as he remembered. One fuel filter light. No problem. He would wait and see what happened next.

The usual chatter filled the radio airwaves. Nothing to worry about.

Kane focused his attention on the instrument panel. Everything was looking good.

The other fuel filter light popped on.

His stomach knotted in about a hundred different ways.

Two fuel filter lights meant fuel contamination. Ugh. The plane had been filled with bad gas.

Kane took a deep breath and exhaled.

Okay, he'd trained for this. He knew what to do.

As he ran through emergency procedures in his head, he flipped to the appropriate section of the flight manual and began the checklist.

Kane radioed his situation to the flight center and was cleared for descent. The only problem would be finding a place to land in the middle of nowhere. If worse came to worst, he could always set down on a freeway or road. Other pilots had done it.

At least the weather was holding. Though while he'd been dealing with his checklist inside the plane, outside the sky had darkened above him. All he needed was clear weather to land this baby. Then the skies could open up with rain, snow, sleet, or all of the above.

He thought about Serena sitting in the back by herself. She would be safer back there. That said, he needed to prepare her for what might happen.

Kane searched for a landing spot as the altimeter spun to a lower altitude, but all he saw were mountains, trees, and canyons. Lots of snow.

Not good.

Over the years, he'd had a few minor incidents in the air and an aborted takeoff, but nothing like this and never with a passenger on board. Definitely not a big-eyed blonde who had looked out of the cockpit window like she was tasting freedom for the first time.

Sweat ran down Kane's spine and slicked his grip on the controls. He flipped on the intercom.

"Listen, Serena," he announced, his voice calm and steady. "You need to prepare for an emergency landing. All items need to be stored securely. That includes in the galley. Once you're done, check your seat belt. Make sure it's flat and tight across your lower torso. When I say 'brace,' I want you to keep your feet flat on the floor and bend forward so you're facing down on your lap. Hold on to your ankles or legs. It might be a little bumpy, but everything will be okay."

Everything would be okay if he could set down before the engines stopped turning.

Unfortunately, with bad fuel, Kane had no idea how long the engines would last.

* * *

Emergency landing?

Every one of Serena's muscles tensed.

Okay, that explained why they were descending. She glanced out the window at the tree-covered, snowcapped mountains. Where were they? Washington? Oregon? Maybe even Idaho?

She didn't understand what was going on, and she didn't like not knowing.

Except for that light, everything seemed fine. Nothing was out of the ordinary except for an edge to Kane's otherwise calm voice—something she hadn't heard before.

Worst-case scenarios bombarded her mind. She tapped her feet, flexed her fingers, and imagined dying.

Don't think about it. Stay in control. Do what Kane told you.

With a plan of action in place, Serena reached for her sketch pad and pencil. With trembling hands, she shoved them into her bag and placed it under a seat. Next, she checked the galley and then her dresses.

Everything seemed okay—secure. Nothing should fly around if they had a rough landing.

Her heart pounded.

She hoped that was all it was.

Focusing on slow, even breaths, Serena sat and tightened her seat belt. She double-checked it, giving the strap one last tug.

Despite that tantalizing interlude in the cockpit, this trip with Tall, Dark, and Sexy had been a mistake. She shivered. She should have stayed firmly on the ground in Boston, where she belonged. Freedom, even a taste of it, wasn't for her. Whether something was wrong with the plane or not, it was too...dangerous.

A strange, whining noise sounded as if something was winding down. She thought about covering her ears but clasped the armrests instead, gripping them so hard her knuckles turned white. An image of Kane, so confident and sure, flying the plane popped into her head, and she felt safer, calmer.

Suddenly, everything went quiet. Too quiet.

Her breath rasped in the silence.

Oh no.

Realization struck, chilling her to the bone. The engines had stopped.

Her jaw clenched.

She stared out the window.

The mountains, so beautiful only moments ago, now loomed dark and deadly below. They seemed closer. The trees taller.

Her heart slammed against her chest.

The plane soared down through the sky, silent as a balsa wood glider.

Fear and panic rioted through her.

Emergency landing? Or a crash landing?

Right now, Serena wasn't sure of anything. She hated the feeling. The lack of control. The whim of fate.

Tears stung her eyes. She'd planned out her entire life, what she wanted and when, but they didn't seem worth much now.

Serena pictured her family and friends. She swallowed around the lump in her throat. She wanted to tell them how much she loved them. She wanted…a second chance.

"Brace!" Kane shouted.

Her heartbeat roaring in her ears, she bent over and grabbed her ankles.

Please let it be over quickly, she prayed.

For a moment, nothing happened. The quiet seemed…unnatural.

Then the plane slammed into the ground. The impact sent her forward against the seat belt, knocking the wind out of her and jostling her around.

Something hit her in the head.

Serena ignored the ache in her stomach, the pain from her head, and the sticky, oozing substance rolling down the side of her face. She concentrated on holding on to her ankles and breathing.

It hurt to breathe.

Kane yelled something. Was he okay?

She struggled for a breath. Yelling was out of the question.

The plane bounced like a ball. Metal shrieked and rattled. The sounds, worse than the crunching of two cars in an accident, made her desperate to cover her ears, but she couldn't let go of her legs.

How much longer?

Make it stop, Kane.

The plane veered and skidded to the right. Serena squeezed her eyes closed and screamed.

CHAPTER FIVE

As a scream from the cabin shivered through the cockpit, Kane broke into a cold sweat. He couldn't think about Serena right now.

He gripped the yoke, his muscles straining to regain control of the speeding plane. The plane jostled, slipping and bouncing on the deceptively flat snow. He couldn't worry about what lay hidden underneath that white blanket. A row of trees loomed straight ahead.

He stepped harder on the brakes.

Come on, baby. Stop for Papa.

The lights on the control panel flickered. What the...

No engines, no electricity, no control.

And Serena was along for the ride.

Kane swore, wrestling the unresponsive yoke as the forest hurtled closer. Individual trees sprang out of the shadowed mass. Far too little space between the solid trunks. Heavy, snow-laden branches. Sharp, frozen pine needles.

Fear was flat and bitter in his mouth.

A hard jolt knocked Kane to the right. He yelled a single word of warning. "Serena!"

His harness held in place. The plane veered, dipped, rolled. The teeth-clenching squeal of tearing metal knotted his stomach.

Time slowed.

Falling sideward, Kane clutched the yoke, his knuckles white, his heart lodged in his throat. The flight manual flew across the cockpit, impacting the window with a loud boom. He expected to be next, but the harness straps dug into his skin, keeping him secured against his seat.

The plane spun, sliding on its side away from the trees, and slowly, ever so slowly, came to a stop.

"Serena?"

A question now. A prayer. A plea.

His pounding heart slammed against his chest. He unbuckled his harness, dropping hard against the center console. He lurched toward the cabin, stumbling over cabinets that now made up the floor. Nothing was where it should be. Light streamed in from the windows above him. Cold air seeped inside from a gash in the fuselage.

Had the tanks ruptured? Was the fuselage or wing on fire?

He didn't smell fuel or smoke, but that didn't mean a fire couldn't start.

His breath steamed in the freezing draft. "Serena?"

"Here."

Her soft voice brought a rush of relief. She drooped at an awkward angle still strapped to her seat. One side of her face was covered in blood. She clutched her stomach.

But she was breathing. Responsive. And unless she'd broken her neck, he had to move her before the plane caught fire—or started sliding into the trees. They could get even more injured if the plane crashed into something else.

After ripping off the bottom of his shirt, he pressed the wadded material to her bleeding scalp.

She gasped in protest.

"Where does it hurt?" he asked, his voice sharp.

"My head and stomach. Ribs, I think." Her voice sounded strained, almost breathless. "Not bad."

Bad enough. "We need to get off the plane. Can you move?"

"I… Yes." Her quiet voice bothered him.

But he had to get her away from the plane in case of a fuel leak or fire. "Good. I'll help you."

Kane reached across her body. His forearm brushed her stomach.

She winced.

"Sorry." Worry made him brusque.

"It's okay."

Kane released the buckle. "Let's go."

She glanced to the back of the cabin. "The wedding dresses."

"There isn't time, Serena." Kane opened the door and stepped out. His feet sank six inches through a crusty layer of snow. No way did he want Serena wading through this.

"This might hurt." He placed one arm around her back and the other under her knees. As he lifted her from the plane, she inhaled sharply.

"Don't apologize," she said.

"I wasn't going to." He carried her from the plane, ignoring the soft curves pressing against him, until he felt they were far enough away in case of an explosion. "Can you stand?"

"Yes." She didn't sound too certain.

Carefully, he placed her on her feet, not letting go until he was sure she wouldn't fall or faint.

"I'm fine." Serena crossed her arms in front of her. "Really."

He took a long look at her. No coat, bleeding head, arms around possibly injured ribs. "You sure have a different definition of 'fine' than I do."

Her gaze dropped.

That wasn't the reaction he wanted. He wanted to rouse her and make her fighting mad. She would need all the fight in her—all her determination and vitality and assurance—to survive this.

"I'll bring back your coat and blankets," he said. "Stay here. I have to check the plane for fuel leaks."

Holding the cloth against her head, Serena nodded gingerly, but her eyes were wide and her face pale. She was injured and scared, and he hated seeing her like this.

His breath hung in the crisp, pine-scented air. He lingered, oddly reluctant to leave her even though he knew what needed to be done. "I'll be right back."

She forced the corners of her mouth upward and made a shooing motion with the hand protecting her ribs. "Go."

That had to hurt her to do, both physically and emotionally, but he appreciated her effort. Not trusting his voice, he nodded and headed to the plane.

A quick but thorough walk-around showed no fuel leaks. Kane checked both engines and the aircraft itself.

The plane lay on its side—crippled and crumpled and torn. Had the landing gear broken and caused the plane to roll? With all these trees in the meadow, he wouldn't have been surprised if they'd hit something. Whatever the reason, the sight in front of him broke his heart.

Everything he had—his livelihood, his home, his love—was gone. Just like that. Just like his mother. He set his jaw.

His life hadn't flashed before his eyes during the crash. But now, Kane saw her, his mother, lying again on the kitchen floor. He'd heard a bang, run downstairs, and found her. Unconscious. Her right hand on her heart. A broken bowl of bread dough beside her.

He'd checked her breathing. None. Her pulse.

None. That hadn't stopped him from calling for help or following the first-aid measures he'd learned over the years, but nothing he did could change the fact it was too late to save her.

Just like it was too late to save the plane.

Kane shook himself. He still needed supplies. Blankets. Serena needed blankets.

He crawled into the plane.

The first stop was the ELT, emergency locator transmitter. Not working.

Kane tried the radio. Nothing. Not even static.

This wasn't looking good.

Sure, he'd radioed his final coordinates, but the plane had drifted several miles while he searched for a safe place to land. The search would start from the last known coordinates and spread out from there. Even if the weather held off, that could mean a long wait before they were found. Especially with this meadow that wasn't big enough to land a plane. They were lucky. So lucky.

They were also missing. Lost. Screwed.

At least he didn't smell fuel.

They could stay inside the plane until they were rescued. Although that tear in the fuselage meant they were in for a long, cold night. He'd have to somehow fix that in the remaining daylight.

Kane scoured the cockpit and cabin, salvaging a first aid kit, flashlight, lighter, food, water, blankets, pillows, and toilet paper from where they'd been tossed and tumbled around the aircraft. He found Serena's purse secured cleverly to the bottom of her seat and then—finally!—her long wool coat buried beneath another seat. Clutching it and a blanket, he trudged through the snow, returning to where he'd left Serena.

Only she wasn't there.

He gripped her coat and the blanket, looking around.

Panic hollowed his gut. "Serena?"

A million and one thoughts screamed through his brain.

Idiot.

He shouldn't have left her alone out here. She had a head injury. Possibly fractured or bruised ribs. Shock. Even the onset of hypothermia.

She couldn't have disappeared in a snow-covered meadow somewhere in middle-of-nowhere Idaho. He noticed a trail of footprints in the snow.

Anger slightly eclipsed his worry.

She could, however, have wandered off.

"Serena?" Kane called her name as he followed her trail to the edge of the meadow where a hillside—more like a mountain—rose steeply.

No way would she have climbed up there. In her condition. In high-heeled boots.

But the footprints led upward. Was she disoriented? Confused? A concussion, maybe.

Or maybe she was just plain dumb.

He climbed up after her. "Serena?"

No answer. He hadn't been gone that long. Five minutes, tops. She couldn't have climbed too high. Unless she'd passed out.

His chest tightened. "Serena?"

"I'm right here." Her low voice sounded almost husky. She carefully made her way down the slope, teetering on her heels in the snow.

He climbed to meet her. Relief at finding her didn't appease his anger. Her face was white, her lips nearly blue.

"What are you doing?" His already skyrocketing blood pressure spiked higher. "I told you to stay put, not walk up a hill. You could have gotten lost or hurt or—"

"I was trying to get a signal on my cell phone." She pulled the hot-pink device out of her pocket, her hands shaking. He was shaking too, from his reaction. "I wanted to call 911."

As if the local fire department could be here in three minutes to help them out of this situation. Kane bundled Serena roughly into her coat and wrapped the blanket over her, hoping she wouldn't notice his trembling hands. "And what if you couldn't find your way back?"

"I picked two spots and made sure I could always see them so I wouldn't get lost. I'm not stupid, Kane."

"I never said—"

But he'd thought it, he realized, chagrined.

She stared up at him, and he found himself...

speechless. He'd always been a pushover for big baby blues, and Serena James had about the prettiest eyes he'd ever seen. Still, he couldn't have her wandering off in the wilderness in her condition.

He looked away, checking her head. At least her scalp wound had stopped bleeding. "You could have gotten disoriented, passed out—"

She arched her eyebrows. "Eaten by bears?"

He scowled. "It's not funny. Too many things can happen out here. We're not in the city anymore. Even if you reached 911, we're a long way from any type of emergency service."

"I just wanted to help."

"Putting yourself in more danger is not helping."

"More danger than, say, being stranded up in the mountains in the middle of a snowstorm?"

"It's not snowing."

She gave him a pointed look. "Yet."

Kane hated to admit it, but she was right. He needed to get them both to shelter before the temperatures dipped further.

"Come on. We'll go back to the plane. The fuselage is damaged, but I can rig something to keep any rain out and block the wind."

"What about the log cabin at the end of the meadow?" she asked.

"What log cabin?"

She pointed. "You can see it from up there."

That could be exactly what they needed. Kane straightened. "Show me."

Tottering on her heels through the snow, she led him a few yards farther up the slope. At the other end of the meadow, a small rustic-looking log cabin was visible through the trees. The kind hunters or hikers might use. Snow drifted across the doorway, but the roof looked solid enough. There appeared to be an outhouse out back. Finally, luck was on their side.

The cabin had to be warmer than the damaged plane.

Especially if those dark clouds overhead decided to drop rain or snow.

"Looks good," he said. "Let's go."

"You're welcome."

"What?" he asked.

"I thought you were thanking me for finding shelter."

"Yeah, I'll be real grateful tonight if the roof doesn't cave in."

"Tonight?" A slight tremor sounded in her voice. Her eyebrows drew together, her forehead wrinkling. "Aren't we going to be rescued soon?"

Not wanting to scare her, he shrugged. "Probably not."

"Aren't you supposed to stay with your vehicle if you're lost?"

"Not if your vehicle won't keep you warm and dry through the night. We can leave a signal," he offered. "An SOS in the snow and an arrow pointing at the cabin in case the searchers arrive at daybreak. The two are close enough together it shouldn't be a problem."

Though the chances of being found tomorrow morning in this kind of weather were slim to none.

The corners of her mouth turned up, and he was glad to see her momentarily appeased.

Serena glanced around. "So what do we do now?"

"We make a signal, gather supplies, and get to the cabin before dark."

Descending the hill, Serena struggled in her heeled boots, but she didn't complain, didn't sigh, didn't grimace. She trudged downward without saying a word.

His respect inched up. She was tough.

More like stubborn, he told himself.

What if she slipped? She could hurt her ribs more or something else.

As she picked her way over a fallen sapling, he grabbed her elbow to steady her. "Watch your step."

She snatched her arm away. "I can manage on my own."

"Yeah, until you fall on that cute bottom of yours."

She glared and marched away, her hips swaying under her brown-and-pink-plaid wool coat.

Stubborn, Kane thought again. But the backside was definitely cute.

* * *

Serena had made enough mistakes in the past seven months to last a lifetime. Stuck there in the middle of who-knew-where, she wouldn't make another. That meant keeping her distance from Kane Wiley. Her boots sank into the snow as she made her way down the mountain.

Being in his arms earlier, feeling the heat and strength emanating from him, had been enough to send her senses spinning. Serena turned up the collar of her coat. Oh, she wanted to blame the reaction on her head injury, on the circumstances surrounding the emergency landing, on the relief of being alive. But she'd felt this way about him before they'd almost died, when she'd been sitting next to him in the cockpit.

The man was as dangerous on the ground as he had been in the air. At least until he started up with the manly, macho I'm-in-charge attitude.

"...until you fall on that cute bottom of yours."

Some nerve, but he was right about the falling part. One wrong step and she could do more than land flat on her face or her bottom. She had no idea if she was concussed or had broken ribs. She might even have other internal injuries. But if so, how would she know?

Unless she wanted Kane to examine her when they reached the cabin.

Serena blew out a frustrated breath. Frustration over the situation, getting hurt and stranded, and Kane himself.

All her plans, so meticulously put together over the years, could literally fall apart because of Kane Wiley. Circumstances could change in an instant. One wrong decision could affect her entire future. That had happened to Morgan when the wrong man had entered her life. Serena wouldn't allow that to happen to her.

With Kane.

"I'm…" *Fine* was on the tip of her tongue once again, but a glimpse at the wilderness surrounding her—natural, raw, untamed—made her feel anything but fine. She had never been more scared in her life, but she'd die before letting Kane know that. She looked at him. "I'm okay."

Or would be, sooner or later.

She hoped.

Right now, she was nothing more than a quivering mass of goo inside. Sheer willpower drove her down this mountainside. Nothing more. And that was, as she'd just told him, okay.

She prided herself on her self-reliance. People counted on her, not the other way around. Serena would never forget what had happened to her sister when she'd given up everything, putting all her faith and trust in one man, the absolutely wrong man for her. Morgan had lost everything, including their parents' love and respect. Years later, her sister was still trying to recover and reinvent herself as she struggled to raise a child on her own. Their parents still hadn't forgiven her lapse in…judgment.

No way did Serena want Kane's assistance. The only thing she needed was a new plan so she could survive this ordeal.

One night in a cabin with him.

No. Big. Deal.

The more times she told herself that, the better.

"Are you warm enough?" he asked.

That depended on the definition of enough. Her feet tingled, the familiar pins-and-needles sensation she got after sitting in one place too long, and her fingers ached. She shoved her hands deeper into her jacket pockets.

That helped. A little.

"Yes," she replied. "Are you?"

"I'm nice and toasty." Kane's mouth curved slightly, and his smile sent a warm rush through her. Too much charm, too little substance. "This little hike has warmed me right up."

She focused on his eyes, serious and intent. "Glad it helped you."

"I'll make an SOS and an arrow pointed at the cabin using rocks and branches. Someone might see it from the air if it doesn't snow."

"I'll help," she offered.

"Your ribs and head."

"If it hurts, I'll stop." Carefully, Serena kneeled, picked up a rock sticking out of the snow, and stood. A knife-edged pain sliced through her midsection. The freezing rock burned her cold hands, causing her to nearly drop it.

"You okay?" Kane asked.

Not trusting her voice, Serena nodded once. She mustered every ounce of strength to carry the rock to where Kane stood without dropping it or crying out.

"Gather tree branches for the arrow." He removed the gloves from his hands. "Put these on."

"I can't take your gloves."

He dropped the pair at her feet and walked away.

Serena stared at the black gloves lying on the snow. She didn't get him. Not at all.

Bending over to pick up the gloves hurt. She had to straighten slowly, but she did and put them on.

As she and Kane worked, the temperature dropped. Finally, both symbols were finished, and it was not a moment too soon. Serena could barely catch her breath. Her ribs hurt so badly. She needed to sit.

"Let's get the supplies from the plane. I'll pull out your suitcase."

"Thanks." Serena wished she were strong enough to get her own bag. Not that any of those clothes packed away were appropriate attire for this weather or situation. Nor were any of them clean. Well, except for a pair of panties. She'd packed an extra. Thank goodness. And then she remembered. "We need to bring the dresses."

"No."

"Yes." She pointed out the tear in the fuselage, not that he was looking at her. "If moisture gets inside the cabin, the dresses could be ruined."

"We can cover them up."

"With what?" Serena mentally counted the days until Calista's wedding. She shuddered. "The dresses must come with us."

"We don't need wedding dresses to survive."

"Belle does."

A beat passed.

"Fine," Kane said. "You want them, you carry them. You'll have to leave your clothes. I'll have my hands full with supplies."

"Fine." Serena felt anything but. Why did he have to be such a jerk about this?

Inside the cabin of the plane, she unhooked the dress bags. She moved slowly to keep from aggravating her sore ribs.

A noise caught Serena's attention. She looked over and found Kane filling a duffel bag with the supplies.

"We need to hurry." He stuffed blankets into the bag. "The sky looks like it's going to open up any minute."

She counted the bags like a mother hen checking her chicks. Six. "I've got them all."

"Come on, then."

Serena struggled to climb out of the plane with the dress bags in her hands.

Kane sighed as if exasperated and took them from her. "Go."

When she was on the ground, he handed over the bulky gowns, tossed down the duffel, and jumped after it.

Serena clutched the bags, unsure what to do with them. She struggled to keep them out of the snow.

Kane lifted another box through the plane's hatch

before closing it behind him. He swung the strap of the duffel bag over his shoulder. "Move it."

He strode in the direction of the cabin, leaving deep tracks in the snow.

Serena stood frozen in place. Between the dresses, her injuries, and the distance she needed to walk, she felt overwhelmed. It wasn't that far, but...

He glanced back. "What are you waiting for?"

Mr. Right.

Someone to take the bags out of her hands, to tell her everything would be okay, and to love her from this day forward no matter what she said or did.

The lump in her throat matched the knot in her heart. Her vision blurred.

Oh no, Serena didn't want to start crying. That wasn't part of their deal. And not part of her image. She stared at the sky, the dark clouds thicker than before, and blinked rapidly.

"Serena?" Kane called.

"I'm coming." What else could she do? Stay here? That would probably please Kane to no end. Blowing out a disgusted breath, she adjusted the bulky bags in her arms. No matter, she could handle this. She would save the dresses herself. Serena walked toward him. "Right behind you."

And that was where she stayed. Behind him.

Keeping up with Kane wasn't easy. Clumsy and hurting, she struggled to walk while holding the bulky dresses. She stumbled in the deep snow, bit back a sigh, and swallowed a cry for help.

She hated every minute of it.

Serena repositioned the dress bags in her arms. The dark sky overhead looked ominous and threatening.

Kane walked back to her. He swore, muttering under his breath. "I knew this would happen."

"I've got them." Well, sort of.

He placed the box on the snow and took the dresses from her. "Carry the supplies."

He trudged toward the cabin without a glance back. The dress bags billowed over his arms as the heavy duffel banged against his hip.

Relieved, she wiped the corner of her eye and picked up the box. She still had trouble walking straight, but the box was lighter and easier to handle than the dress bags.

No matter what she might have thought of him, attractive or not, a gentleman or a ladies' man, a nice guy or a jerk, he had saved the dresses by carrying them. Serena would toast Kane at the upcoming poker and margarita night they held each month. The next one, she remembered with a pang, would also be a surprise bridal shower for Calista at Rebecca's house.

Calista.

Serena had to keep her gown safe.

Halfway to the cabin, a mix of sleet and snow poured from the sky, stinging her cheeks and chilling her lungs. The scent of ice permeated the air.

Forget that it was only November—winter had arrived. Those dress bags had better be waterproof as advertised.

With each step, the conditions deteriorated. Damp hair clung to her face. Her jacket felt heavier. The box in her hands weighed her down. She had no sense of direction.

"We're almost there!" Kane yelled. "Do you see the cabin?"

She scanned the horizon, but all she could see was white in every direction. A burst of panic rioted through her. "No."

"Eleven o'clock."

Serena squinted in that direction. More white. And then the roofline came into focus.

Thank goodness. "I see it."

"Don't lose sight of the cabin."

She didn't want to lose sight of him. A bone-deep chill overtook her, making breathing and walking harder, but she forged ahead, propelled by fear and responsibility. Her numb fingers, in their borrowed gloves, cried out in pain. Guiltily, she wondered how Kane's hands were faring, especially while carrying the gowns.

The gowns.

If Serena couldn't get to the cabin and Kane was forced to backtrack to her with the dresses, they would get wetter. She quickened her pace.

And fell flat on her bottom.

Just as Kane had predicted she would.

She sat on the snow empty-handed and struggled to breathe. "Please don't turn around."

He didn't.

Kane reached the cabin and pushed his shoulder against the door. A banging sound echoed.

If he opened the door, he would look back.

Every muscle ached. Her ribs hurt. She couldn't catch her breath, but her pride was stronger than her physical ailments.

Using every ounce of strength she could muster, Serena climbed to her feet. Pain radiated through her stomach. She waited for the hurt to subside, then brushed the snow off her bottom.

Thank goodness Kane was still trying to get into the cabin. Each attempt boomed through the meadow.

She gathered the supplies that had fallen onto the snow, put them back into the box, and marched to the cabin, using sheer willpower.

By the time she arrived, the door was open. Kane stood outside, brushing the snow and ice off the dress bags.

"The dresses," she said.

"Get inside."

His harsh tone made her wince. The sound matched his dark eyes.

Serena did as she'd been told without a word. She surmised from the musty smell that no one had been inside in weeks, maybe months.

She placed the box of supplies on a wooden table with chairs pushed under it. Her breath hung on the cold, stale air. The temperature inside the one-room cabin was warmer than outside, but not by much, so she left her wet coat on.

Kane stepped inside. He hung the dress bags on one of the two sets of metal bunk beds along the wall opposite the door. Four beds, but only one mattress.

She gulped. What had she gotten herself into?

"There must be a propane tank somewhere for the two wall lamps, the stovetop, and the oven." He removed the duffel bag from around his shoulder and picked up some sort of tube on the table. "I need to check the chimney so we can use the woodstove and remove the shutters to get some air and light in here. I'll be right back."

Serena stood in near darkness. She noticed a wood cupboard, opened it up, and found cans of food. Not quite all the comforts of home, but they would be warm here and wouldn't starve. If you didn't mind rustic, the cabin was almost quaint and cozy with its log walls, beamed ceilings, and small, wood-paned windows. With the right companion, one might even find the place romantic.

Noises sounded on the roof and then on the two sides of the cabin with windows.

Several long minutes later, Kane returned, carrying a stack of wood. He pulled his jacket off and hung it on a hook behind the door.

"No leaking holes in the roof, unlike my plane." As Kane opened the door to the stove, the hinges creaked. "Ya done good, Blondie."

Serena swallowed. "You, too."

"We're in this together."

She nodded.

He grabbed pieces of paper from the duffel bag, crumpled up a few pages, and stuck them inside the stove. Next, he added a few smaller logs from the stash of dry wood sitting next to the stove, pulled out a lighter from a pocket in his bag, and lit the paper on fire.

The burst of heat warmed her from five feet away. The crackling sound and smell of burning wood filled the air.

Serena would never take central heating for granted again. She removed the wet gloves.

"Stand closer to the stove," he suggested.

She did, placing her icy hands over the top. As the heat warmed her fingers, she wiggled all ten digits. "Thanks."

Next, he lit the two wall lamps, filling the cabin with light. Kane didn't stop there. He poured a bottle of water into a pot on the stovetop. "You'll feel better once you drink something hot."

"What about you?" she asked, knowing he had to be as cold as she was.

He kicked his shoes off and removed his socks. "Let's get you warmed up first."

His concern for her well-being surprised Serena. He didn't seem the nurturing type. Despite his attitude, she hated being forced to depend on him for, well, everything.

A gust of wind rattled the windows. She shivered. If only the storm would go away so they could be found...

"You've done a great job getting us set up here." And she meant that. Serena was relieved he was with her.

Not many men—definitely not Rupert, who watched home improvement shows with her but didn't own a toolbox, or Malcolm, who got weekly manicures—would know what to do in a situation like this. Rupert would go crazy without being able to use his cell phone or laptop. Malcolm would be so inspired by the surroundings to design a line of casual outerwear he wouldn't worry about anything else, including survival.

At least Kane, the poster boy for Mr. Oh-So Wrong, knew how to get them through a whiteout, break into the cabin, and get a fire going so they would have a warm, dry place to stay tonight. Yes, she could have been in worse hands. An unfamiliar yet content feeling settled over her.

"Warmed up enough?" Kane asked.

"For what?"

"To get undressed."

CHAPTER SIX

Kane scowled, feeling like an idiot for what he'd said. Still, he wasn't about to admit that. A jerk move, probably.

Serena wrapped her arms over her chest. "Get undressed?"

"You're not that irresistible, babe." Yes, he was being a jerk, but she didn't seem to understand their situation. "We need to get out of our wet clothes to avoid hypothermia. That's all."

With the dried blood on her forehead and her face, she looked as if she'd fought a long, hard battle. Still, she raised her chin. "I don't have any other clothes to wear."

Serena had been polite up until now. Stubborn, yes, but composed. He appreciated her poise. She'd even tried to lift rocks with her ribs hurting. Kane respected that. But the way she stared down her nose at him like some ice princess irritated him. The last thing he wanted, the last thing he needed, was to be responsible for someone else, especially a wide-eyed blonde who reminded him of his worst mistakes.

"You've got six wedding dresses to choose from," he said. "Take your pick."

Her mouth gaped. She tried to speak, but no words came out.

He'd stunned her into silence, but he was only telling her the truth. "You chose the gowns over your clothes. Someone should get some use out of them."

"Someone will. The very lucky women I designed them for." Her eyes never left his. "Which is why I refuse to parade around a dirty, cold cabin in a couture wedding gown."

"Fine." Kane had just been rattling her chain, anyway. He opened the jam-packed duffel bag, pulled out a blanket and a shirt, and tossed them to her. "Here."

"You want me to wear these?"

"It's all we've got. I left most of my clothes on the plane to bring supplies." Kane failed to mention he'd only brought clothes for himself. He wasn't used to thinking about someone else. "I also have pants if you want them."

"That's okay. I don't need to change." She flapped the sides of her skirt like a flamenco dancer. "I'm drying off."

"Yeah, right." Her coat looked like a sopping-wet, oversized dishrag. Droplets fell from the hem of her skirt. Her sad excuse for boots were waterlogged. Not good for warming her up. "Take off your clothes, or I'll take them off for you."

Her eyes widened. "What did you say?"

"You heard me." He opened the first aid kit he'd packed in the duffel bag. "Hypothermia is nothing to mess around with. Your speech slurs, your breathing slows down, your skin becomes pale and cold, you shiver uncontrollably, and you feel lethargic and confused. In its final stages, you feel so hot you rip your clothes off to cool down. But by then, it's usually too late."

"Too late?"

"To recover."

A beat passed. She tried to remove her coat, wincing with every movement.

After her third attempt, Kane swore under his breath. He did not need this—her. He grabbed hold of the jacket's collar.

"You're going to hurt yourself more." Carefully, he drew the coat down her arms and over her hands.

She didn't grimace, but he could tell she was in pain.

He put the jacket on another hook on the back of the cabin door. "This thing weighs a ton. I can't believe you hiked all the way here wearing it."

"I didn't have a choice."

"True, but you're stronger than you look."

"Thank you," she mumbled even though she looked too far gone with her injuries to be that polite.

"Sit." He moved an empty chair closer to the stove. "I'll take your boots off. Then you can undress."

Serena sat still and silent as if waiting for a jury to declare her innocence or guilt. She clutched the blanket and the shirt in her lap.

"Left or right?" Kane asked.

She raised her right foot, and he pulled on her tall boot. The wet leather clung to her slender calf and didn't budge. She gripped the seat of the chair.

"This might hurt," he said.

"Just get them off." A hint of vulnerability flickered in her eyes. "Please."

Her plea hit him hard in the gut.

"You got it." Kane peeled the leather off, folding it over toward her ankle. He tugged until the boot came off. "Next."

She raised her left foot. Removing that one was easier now that he knew what to do.

"Now your"—he stared at her feet—"tights?"

As she reached under her skirt, he stared dumbfounded. What was she doing? He tilted his head.

Serena rolled something down her leg. "Thigh highs."

Despite the chill lingering in the air and his wet clothes, his temperature shot up twenty degrees. Time to get back to business. "I need to check your ribs."

"My ribs are better."

"Your breathing's off."

"Do you make a habit of staring at women's chests?"

94

"Every chance I get," he admitted cheerfully. "Come on. Let's have a look."

Her mouth tightened. "You're a pilot, not a doctor."

"Right," he acknowledged. "But I've played doctor before."

Serena stared at him.

Okay, he would cut her some slack for having no sense of humor, given the circumstances. "You like being in control and taking care of yourself, right?"

She nodded.

"I'm the same way. I'm used to being on my own and not having to worry about anyone else. But sometimes life throws you a curveball, and you have to make the best of it. I'm all you've got, Blondie," he said. "So lift your shirt."

"Does that line ever work?"

"You'd be amazed."

"I'd be astonished." A corner of her mouth lifted. "You really need to work on your bedside manner."

Finally, a crack in the princess's ice.

He bit back a smile. "You think?"

"Most definitely." Serena raised her blouse enough to show an inch of smooth skin and a flat stomach.

Oh man. Attraction hit hard. His mouth went dry. He focused on her belly button—an innie—to keep his gaze from wandering.

"Kane?"

What was he doing? Staring? Leering?

Talk about a curveball. She was his passenger. His responsibility. He was stuck taking care of her whether he liked it or not. "Where does it hurt?"

Serena pointed to her left side. "Here."

He studied the spot, trying to ignore her creamy complexion and the curve of her waist. He pressed lightly. Her skin was soft against his fingers, but then he saw a small laceration, most likely from the seat belt. "Does this hurt?"

"A little."

He moved toward her ribs where the skin was already bruising. He would need to be careful how he touched her. "How about here?"

She winced. "Ouch."

Kane pulled his hand back. "I—"

"It's okay," she said before he could apologize. "Really."

"You could have fractured a rib, but they're likely just bruised. There's no way to tell without an X-ray." He just hoped there weren't any internal injuries. He opened the first aid kit, which was fully stocked. At least he was prepared. "The seat belt left a cut. I'll clean and bandage it, but I want to wrap your ribs first to be on the safe side. Stand up."

She did and raised her blouse higher. He glimpsed the lace edge of her bra—pink, but who was noticing?—and sucked in a breath.

Don't look. Don't think. Just get it done.

Wrapping the bandage around her ribs, he focused

on mentally reciting the multiplication tables for nine, ten, and eleven. "How does that feel? Too tight?"

She looked as uncomfortable as he felt. "Just right."

Was it? Kane hoped so. He didn't want to hurt her.

He secured the end, cleaned the laceration, added antibiotic cream, and covered the spot with a large bandage. "All done."

"Thanks," she murmured.

Outside, the storm raged, and the wind blew. Icy pellets hit the cabin, sounding like marbles being dropped on the roof and thrown at the windows. The forced intimacy of the situation only added to the tension inside. The lack of conversation didn't help. The burning logs crackled. The water boiled. The sound and sight of their breaths filled the air.

It had been a long day. It would be an even longer night.

"Now, let's take care of the cut on your forehead." He washed away the dried blood with an antiseptic wipe, dabbed antibiotic cream on the cut, and placed two butterfly bandages over the long gash. She didn't flinch or complain. "All done. It's not too bad, but you might have a little scar."

"A scar?" She sounded concerned.

"Maybe, right near your temple. It's hard to tell."

She reached up, but he grabbed her hand.

"Don't touch."

"But—"

"A little vitamin E oil can go a long way." He released her hand. "Though guys dig chicks with scars."

"Not all men. Some leave at the first sight of an imperfection."

"Idiots," Kane muttered. "You'd be better off without a man like that. Scars show a person takes risks and isn't afraid to live. Very cool in my book."

She gazed up at him. "You mean that?"

"Yep."

A shy smile graced her lips. "Thanks."

"No problem." He grabbed the dry pants—a pair of khakis. "You want them?"

"No, thanks," she said. "I'll stick with what I have."

"You can stay here by the stove. I'll change over there by the bunk beds."

He unbuckled his belt and unzipped his pants. As he pulled them off, he heard another zipper—Serena's skirt?—and the rustling of fabric.

"If something's even just damp, take it off." He removed his underwear and torn shirt. "We can hang our clothes on the hooks and purlins so they'll be dry in the morning."

"Okay."

Kane almost laughed. Nothing about this was okay, especially standing naked in a cold cabin, miles away from civilization, with a beautiful woman he wanted nothing to do with. He pulled on the dry pants and zipped them. "You dressed?"

The sound of fabric ripping filled the air. "Almost."

The scent of smoke lingered in the air even though he'd opened the damper to the flue. Staring at the cabin's aged, dark wood walls, Kane wondered who else had been forced to take refuge there during a winter storm. The items inside—food and firewood—suggested someone used the cabin. Maybe forest service employees checked the place routinely. He hoped that was the case, or they could be stuck there for a long time.

"I'm dressed," Serena said.

Kane turned. His mouth dropped open. Unbelievable. She looked like a Grecian princess with the blanket wrapped around her body and tied at the waist and at the top with sashes made from strips of fabric. Absolutely beautiful.

"Wow." Forget about being cold. His temperature shot into the red zone. He remembered what she'd said about her dresses. "You can even make 'couture' out of a blanket."

"What can I say?" She had slipped on his blue shirt, buttoned the front, and rolled up the sleeves. The color brought out the blue of her eyes. "It's a gift."

Seeing her wearing his shirt was kind of sexy, too. "I'd say so."

He smiled at her.

She smiled back.

In that moment, time stopped and they could have

been anywhere—the cabin, inside the plane, Seattle, Boston. The place didn't matter.

Only here, only now, only them.

The beat of his heart seemed stronger, the blood flowing through his veins warmer. He didn't want to have to take care of her. He didn't want to have to worry about her. But he wouldn't have wanted to be with anyone else.

The moment lingered.

Kane knew he should break the eye contact, but he didn't want to. He hadn't felt this connected to someone in…well, ever.

Finally, Serena looked away, resting her gaze on the bunks for a few seconds before focusing on the woodstove. "I guess there's not much else to do except hit the sack. I mean, bed. You know, sleep. Somewhere."

She looked cute, all flustered with her cheeks pink. Forget the ice princess glare or the Grecian princess attire—she was suddenly natural and approachable.

Too bad she was practically engaged or something.

"You can always make a nest out of those wedding dresses," he said to lighten the mood and set some distance between them. "Lots of nice, comfy material there."

But instead of getting all prissy on him again, Serena laughed. "Obviously, you don't know much about wedding gown fabrics. Tulle is too scratchy, and satin is too slippery. Silk wouldn't be too bad except for all the beading and appliqué. That would be uncomfortable."

His smile widened. "Then we'll have to share the bed."

* * *

Serena had been afraid he'd say that.

"You have a boyfriend," Kane finished for her. "I understand."

But she didn't. And he couldn't.

"Using our body heat is the best way to keep each other warm," he explained.

The coal-sized lump in her throat kept her from answering.

"You can trust me, Serena."

But the real question was: Did she trust herself? Serena had never understood what unknown trait made a totally wrong man so irresistible to a woman. She had vowed never to allow herself to be in that position, never to make the same mistake her sister had.

Which meant figuring out how to handle this…dilemma. Serena fussed with the folds of the blanket she wore.

"Hungry?" he asked.

She nodded, rolling up the long-sleeved shirt more. Wearing Kane's shirt felt strange, and she wasn't sure she liked it.

He unwrapped the cellophane from a sandwich. "Turkey and Swiss cheese okay?"

"My favorite, actually." She stared at the sandwich he placed in front of her. "Thanks."

He sat at the table with a sandwich of his own. "We have two more sandwiches, a bunch of fruit, and enough prepackaged snacks to last a week."

"Plus all the canned goods I found in the cupboard. We won't starve."

They ate quickly without saying a word. She didn't mind the silence. Not when she needed to figure out a solution to their sleeping arrangement problem. One that didn't involve a long, cold night shivering on the table or floor. She had to think of something.

The alternative...

Serena didn't want to feel Kane's bare, broad shoulders and chest against her. She didn't want to feel his heart beating. She didn't want to inhale his warm breath. Smelling his scent was bad enough. Those things were too intimate, too dangerous.

"What if we slept head to toe in the opposite direction?" she suggested. "We'd still be able to share body heat, but not..."

Time to stop babbling. The less she said, the better. A mouse scurried across the floor. She didn't scream, but she lifted her feet.

"Not a bad suggestion," he said, not seeming to notice the mouse. "But you don't want your nose anywhere near my feet. Besides, we'll still be in contact no matter which direction we face."

"True." She rubbed her hands together. "I'm just..."

"Nervous?"

"A little." *More like a lot.* "Silly, I know."

He pulled out another blanket. "Once you feel how warm it is when we're both in bed, all your doubts will disappear."

She was afraid of that.

Still, Serena knew he was right. Keeping warm was the most important thing.

She slowly crawled onto the lower bunk, trying to breathe through the pain. The mattress, more like a pad, sank from her weight.

"Give me a shove if I snore," he joked.

"Uh, sure." She didn't want to touch him, let alone shove him. "But I'm so tired I probably won't notice anything."

Facing the log wall, she squeezed her eyes shut. She wanted sleep to come quickly and easily tonight.

Something creaked. The floor? The roof? Something bigger than a mouse?

She opened her eyes to total darkness as if the moon and stars had been sucked into a vacuum. She couldn't see her hand. He must have turned off the lamps.

Serena lay there. She smelled smoke and heard the burning logs in the stove. She also felt a presence nearby.

Kane.

The mattress sank to the right. He crawled in.

His foot brushed hers, and tingles shot up her leg. She stiffened.

"Oops," he said.

The tingles didn't stop. She swallowed. "It's a little cramped."

He shrugged. "Better than the floor."

"Or a chair." She didn't want to sound as if she were complaining. He shouldn't have to put up with that after today, even if she only wanted to fly home on a wide-body plane with four engines, at least two pilots, and three hundred passengers.

Far away from this wilderness nightmare. Far, far away from Kane.

"It could be worse," he said.

She rolled toward him. "What?"

"It could be worse," Kane repeated.

The wind howled, blowing snow against the cabin, the noises outside as unfamiliar as the complete darkness inside. Thinking about the emergency landing sent a chill shivering down her spine. This couldn't be any worse unless one of them had been seriously injured. "Thank you for landing the plane, Kane, and coming after me and…"

"Just doing my job." He sounded so nonchalant after saving their lives.

"It was more than that."

"You've done well yourself. Finding this cabin."

"Sure beats the airplane."

"I'll say." He rolled onto his side. The motion sent her falling back against him. She scooted away. Well, as far away as she could manage on a twin-size bed. "But you would have managed in the plane tonight if it had come to that."

"No, I wouldn't have," she whispered. Immediately, Serena cringed. She couldn't believe she'd said the words out loud.

His body drew closer. "Why do you say that?"

She was afraid to move. Breathe. "It's just—"

"What?"

This was so hard, but she felt like she owed it to him to be a little vulnerable after all he'd done for her today. "I'm not exactly the type to just go with the flow without quite a bit of...planning and preparation."

"You've been doing okay here with very little prep time."

His compliment pleased her. More than it should. "Thanks."

"You're welcome. I'm more a fly-by-the-seat-of-my-pants type of guy."

"I like to go where I want to go."

She remembered what he'd said in the cockpit about his need for freedom. "We're very different."

"Yes, we are."

His words saddened her for some reason.

Isolated by the snow and wilderness, cut off from everything and everyone familiar, she wanted to be like Kane. If she could be more like him, their circumstance might not be so hard to handle.

"We'll get through this," he reassured. "Go to sleep."

Not such an easy thing to do when lying next to him felt so good. Better than it should.

His body heat warmed the space next to her. The rasp of his breathing and the beat of his heart told her she wasn't entirely alone. Letting her guard down and drifting off to sleep probably wasn't the smartest course of action.

Not when she felt safe and secure with Kane. Two ways she never thought she'd ever feel with a man like him, someone who didn't match her at all. They might have been different, but those differences made her feel better and more at ease.

Out here where she didn't belong, Serena knew he would take care of her. Make sure they survived. She survived. Whether she wanted his help or not.

And for that, she was grateful.

More than he would ever know.

GROUP CHAT #3

8:00 PM Pacific Time

Kelsey: *Are you home yet, Serena?*
Elle: *She should be unless they ran into delays.*
Jane: *I tried calling, but it went straight to voicemail. I bet she's still in Airplane Mode.*

11:00 PM Pacific Time

Kelsey: *Still no Serena.*
Elle: *She usually checks in.*
Jane: *Still going to voicemail. Maybe her battery died.*
Kelsey: *It's late in Boston, but I'll call Belle in the morning if we don't hear from Serena.*
Elle: *She'll laugh when she reads these messages.*
Jane: *And we'll laugh when she replies.*

7:00 AM Pacific Time

Kelsey: *Serena didn't show up to work this morning. Belle reached out to the pilot's father, and they discovered the flight never landed in Boston last night.*

Elle: *Where are they?*

Kelsey: *The plane's last known position places them somewhere over Idaho.*

Jane: *Last known position?*

Kelsey: *Kane and Serena's plane is officially missing.*

Elle: *Oh, no! I can't believe this is happening. I'm praying they're okay.*

Kelsey: *I'm calling my uncle. Will is reaching out to people too.*

Jane: *So we just have to wait for news?*

Kelsey: *For now. Unfortunately.*

CHAPTER SEVEN

Half asleep, Kane snuggled against the inviting warmth and feminine softness of the body beside him. He could have gotten used to waking up like this. She had her back against his chest and her feet tucked between his legs. He enjoyed having his legs tangled in hers, and her floral scent made him want to inhale deeply.

His hand rested on the curve of her hip. The fabric of her makeshift skirt was all that separated skin from skin. His eyes fluttered open, but he didn't move. Not even his hand.

Serena.

Waking up with her so close in this small bed was...nice.

Yeah, nice.

As if he were sleeping with a cuddly puppy or something. A puppy would have been better than an attractive woman with a serious boyfriend. What was he thinking? Doing?

He untangled himself and crawled off the lower bunk.

A faint light shone through the paned windows.

Morning already? Kane felt as if he'd only closed his eyes a few moments ago.

Outside, a blanket of fresh white powder covered the ground, trees, and bushes, the entire scene like a Christmas card even though that holiday wouldn't happen for more than a month.

Pain ricocheted through Kane's chest as he remembered Christmases with Mom. She would have been frantic right now if she were alive and knew he was missing. He thought about his father. Had Dad been notified of the situation? Were people searching for them yet? Would Belle know that something was wrong when Serena didn't show up for work this morning?

The overcast skies this morning didn't fill Kane with much hope for rescue, but at least the snow had stopped. Their SOS could have been covered, though. He might as well take advantage of the break in the weather and return to the plane to see. Maybe he could bring more supplies back to the cabin, too.

With the hint of a smile on her face, Kane wondered what she might be dreaming about. Shopping and weddings? Or something more, deeper, secret?

Unexpected warmth settled over him, but he shook it off.

He dressed in his clothes from yesterday, now dry. Then, after adding a log to the woodstove so she wouldn't wake up cold, he put his shoes on.

"Where are you going?" Serena asked softly.

"To the plane. It's stopped snowing. I'm going to check on our signal and bring back more supplies. Clothes."

She sat up on her elbows, looking sleep rumpled and adorable. "Want me to go with you?"

"Stay here. You can help me later, okay?"

Serena nodded.

"How are your ribs?" he asked.

"Not as sore."

"Good. Probably bruised, then, and not broken," he said, relieved she felt better. "Go back to sleep."

She closed her eyes and rolled over to face away from him.

Kane watched her for a moment, noticing her long, graceful neck, considering her curves under the blanket and how he'd been the big spoon to her little spoon. He shook the memory off and headed outside, where the cold would do him some good.

He hiked back to the plane, his steps sinking into the newly fallen snow, unable to follow his and Serena's footprints from yesterday due to the weather overnight.

Not a good sign.

At the plane, he couldn't see the SOS or the arrow. He spent five minutes trying to locate the rocks and branches and another ten brushing and kicking the snow off. Given the thick, dark-cloud-covered sky, his effort felt like a lesson in futility since it would start snowing any minute now. But if Serena asked about the signals, he wanted to be able to tell her the truth.

Who knew? Maybe a plane was looking for them right now.

The thought made him light a fire in the middle of the snow-covered meadow, far away from any trees or plants. Smoke might be easier for others to see than the SOS, arrow, or fuselage.

As smoke drifted up to the sky, Kane focused on the plane. Snow coated the crippled aircraft, and he swore under his breath.

He'd known that the damage had been bad, but seeing the plane this morning… He wanted to punch something.

Disappointment crashed into him. Frustration burned acridly. He'd lost everything.

No, not everything.

He was still there. Serena, too. No reason to lose control.

Kane entered the plane through the gash and looked for anything useful, including the clothes he'd removed from his duffel bag yesterday. He found his camera in the pile and took pictures of the plane in case the insurance company needed them. By the time he had finished and closed the door to the plane, snowflakes fell from the sky and the fire was dying.

So much for a break in the weather.

Kane unloaded Serena's suitcase and his second bag. He noticed items from the bridal show. He remembered the candles from the booth and took out the two boxes. There might have been other stuff they could use. Something that might make Serena more comfortable. Besides, he should take everything he could. This might be his last trip back to the plane today.

The snow fell faster, harder.

Or tomorrow.

* * *

Serena stared out of the cabin window. With all the white on the ground and more falling from the sky, she couldn't see anything, including Kane. Her pulse quickened, or maybe that was a shot of adrenaline. "Where are you?"

She rubbed her arms to fight a shiver. She'd changed into her own clothes. Wearing Kane's shirt had felt too intimate, but now, she wanted to put it on again. Anything to feel closer to him. She didn't like being left alone. Who was she kidding? She didn't like any of this.

Not that she was throwing herself a pity party.

That wasn't her style. She'd done a couple of things this morning: visited the outhouse, tried to find reception on her cell phone, brushed her teeth, and set out a breakfast of fruit, granola bars, and raisins.

She thought about checking the wedding dresses, but she didn't want to expose them to the smoke smell or the mice she'd seen. It was safer to leave them zipped in the bags where they would be safe.

But with Kane gone for so long and the weather turning bad again, she could only wait and worry. What if he didn't come back?

Needing to do something to distract herself, she forced herself away from the window, organized the food, and tidied the cabin the best she could. But thoughts of Kane never left her mind. "Come back to me, please."

The minutes dragged on, and her anxiety rose.

Finally, a noise sounded outside. The storm or...

Please be him.

Serena opened the door. A gust of wind blew snow and cold air inside, pushing the door into the cabin. She didn't care. Not when she saw Kane pulling her suitcase like a sled through the snow. Piled on top were boxes and a duffel bag.

Relief flooded her, but she played it cool. Easy to do with the snow falling hard and fast.

Goose bumps prickled her skin. She should have put on her coat, but seeing him sent warmth surging through her veins. "Back already?"

"You're going to get cold." His mouth tightened. "Where are your coat and shoes?"

Why had she wanted him to come back? Serena sighed. "I want to help. Hand me something."

He hesitated and then handed her one of the smaller boxes. "Watch your ribs."

"They don't hurt as much today, but I'll be careful." She helped him unload, but only the lighter supplies. Together, they moved everything inside in two trips.

Kane closed the door, shutting out the storm and sealing them inside. "Thanks for the help."

With his rugged good looks, razor stubble on his face, and strong body, he looked like a renegade mountain man. Rough, raw, wild. All he needed was a rifle, boots, and a parka to complete the picture.

"You're welcome." Serena fought the urge to brush the snow from his hair. Personality aside, even a casual touch wouldn't have been a good idea. He might not have been the kind of man she wanted in her life, but she couldn't deny his physical appeal. "You brought back a lot of stuff."

"It'll save me a trip later."

"Smart thinking." And that would save her from worrying about being alone again. "But it's almost like moving day with all these things crammed in here."

"Did you just move?"

"About a year ago. I have a condo in Back Bay."

He unpacked one of the boxes. "Must be nice."

"It is, but I'd rather have a house. One with a fireplace, a fenced yard, a sewing room, and"—*a nursery*—"room for a family."

Serena ignored the twinge of disappointment that

115

her plans weren't going accordingly right now. And hadn't been for a while.

"What about you?" It hurt when she bent over, but that didn't stop her from rummaging through her suitcase for warmer clothing. "Where do you live?"

"As of now, here."

Oops. She gave him a sheepish smile. "Oh, right. Sorry."

Kane added a log to the fire. "What's with the food?"

Didn't he like it? Had she wasted their provisions? Or did he think she was trying too hard, like a woman who slipped from her lover's bed to make him pancakes?

Of course, Kane probably liked pancakes. Serena would have settled for coffee.

She lifted her chin. "While you were gone, Bigfoot made breakfast."

"Looks good." Kane's grin reached his eyes. "Thanks, Sasquatch."

Okay, Serena felt better. Except her tummy felt all tingly. Hungry. She must have been hungry.

She recognized boxes from the bridal show. "Why did you bring these back?"

"To see if we could find anything useful inside." He bit into a granola bar.

She opened the first box and dug through the contents. Jackpot. "Oh. Wow."

"Candles?"

116

"Something better. Something you're going to like."

He popped a grape into his mouth. "What's that?"

She raised a small item wrapped in cellophane from the box. "Chocolate."

He wiped his hand over his forehead in an exaggerated gesture. "Now I can last at least another day."

Serena pulled out the pieces and placed them on the table. "We have enough for a few more days if worse comes to worst."

"Someone will come for us."

His words reassured her and gave her hope. "As soon as the weather breaks."

A slight hesitation and then he nodded.

Uh-oh. "What's wrong?" she asked.

"Nothing's wrong. But finding us might take a few days even after the weather breaks."

Days, as in plural. She chewed on the inside of her cheek.

"It'll be okay, Serena."

"I'm sure things will be better now that you've found chocolate." She hoped she sounded lighthearted and cheerful despite the heaviness pressing down on her chest.

"Much better."

Serena nodded. This was so outside the norm for her, and she missed her ordinary everyday routine and comforts of home. A picnic was about the closest she'd come to the outdoors in the past ten years. "We have plenty of water to drink with all the snow."

"Just remember, don't eat the snow. Otherwise, your body wastes too many calories trying to melt it."

"How do you know all this?" she asked, impressed.

"I was a Boy Scout."

"Interesting." She tried and failed to picture him fresh-faced with neatly trimmed hair and a sharply pressed uniform. Though she could imagine him being a cute little boy. "The Scouts seem like they would have been too structured for someone like you."

"Like me?"

"A free spirit."

"I was just a kid. I didn't know the meaning of the word *free*. Scouting was what my dad and I did together back then."

"You must have had fun. Charlie's a great guy."

"He has his moments."

She thought about Kane's father and how he had wanted to buy Belle's late husband's old car. Even after she'd said no, Charlie kept coming around the shop, which was how they started dating. "He seems to be really taken with Belle."

"My father goes after what he wants. No matter the consequences."

The bitterness lacing Kane's words surprised her. "Charlie doesn't seem like he has tunnel vision to me. He was okay when Belle wouldn't sell her car to him."

Kane shrugged.

"Either way," Serena said. "He must be so worried about you right now."

"Maybe. We aren't that close anymore. I don't see him much when I'm in Boston. Sometimes not at all."

She didn't understand. "But he's your father."

"He's done a few things I don't agree with."

Serena got a familiar sinking feeling in her stomach. "So, what? You stay away from him because of that?"

Kane nodded. "He made his choices. He can live with the consequences."

Her heart dropped. Kane was just like her parents, who withheld love if they were disappointed. That was so unfair, so wrong. Serena had tried to make her parents see what they were doing, but they wouldn't listen. Maybe she could help Kane see what he was doing by holding a grudge. "I'm sure your father is frantic right now."

With a shrug, Kane finished his granola bar. "I'd bet Rupert is more worried about you."

Serena stared out the window. The news would only bring relief to her ex-boyfriend. No more bumping into her at the newest café or hippest club with a date by his side and dealing with the ensuing awkwardness.

"Rupert…" Guilt coated her mouth at the thought of lying again. Her friends, her family, even Kane deserved better.

"What?" Kane asked.

The silence tightened the knot in her stomach. She

119

listened to her breathing, to his, to the logs popping in the wood stove. "We're not... We... Rupert broke up with me."

There. She'd said it. And surprisingly, her world hadn't imploded.

Instead, a rare peace filled her heart. Finally, someone knew the truth.

His eyes darkened. "Belle said—"

"No one knows."

"Why not?"

"Well...not telling anyone made sense at the time." Serena took a deep breath and exhaled slowly. "I planned to tell people, but I never found the right opportunity. Everyone was so happy about our florist's upcoming wedding. I didn't want my news to spoil the fun. And one of my college besties got married this year, and I didn't want her to worry. And another one of my college friends was cheated on right before her wedding, so I didn't want to add to her heartache." Serena watched the snow falling from the sky. Each flake reminded her of the time that had passed. "And soon, the days turned into weeks, so telling them seemed like an even bigger deal than before."

"Your friends won't care."

But Serena cared. She didn't want their sympathy or their pity. She only wanted them to see her as a smart, successful woman on her way to having it all. "They'll be disappointed."

He raised his eyebrows. "All because you aren't practically engaged?"

"Because I'm not"—*perfect*—"the person they thought I was."

The person they liked. The person they depended on. The person she had taught herself to be. Bright, capable, and accomplished, without needs or flaws.

"What about The Suit?" Kane asked.

"The Suit?" And then she remembered. "Malcolm is a friend who would like for us to become business partners."

"He wants more than that," Kane said. "And you?"

"I…" She thought about Malcolm. She couldn't ask for anything more in a man on paper, but she only thought of him as a friend. And though he was a great guy, she wasn't sure what kind of father he'd be. Dad potential was an important quality for her Mr. Right. "Probably not."

"So no boyfriend?"

"No boyfriend." Serena stared at the windowsill, where a heart was carved into the wood with little initials engraved. She traced the letters with her fingertip. Maybe V and J had found the true love she wanted so badly. "Pretty pathetic, huh?"

"That you don't have a boyfriend?"

Not having a boyfriend didn't bother her as much as how not having a boyfriend affected her plans. She shook her head. "That I lied."

"Not lied. More like withheld information." Kane rose from his chair. "You had your reasons."

"It seemed so at the time."

He moved toward her with purpose and intent. "You did it for your friends."

"I did."

"You weren't trying to hurt anyone." He stopped in front of her. "You wanted to help them by making sure they were happy."

"You nailed it." A smile tugged on the corners of her mouth. "And you also made me feel better. Thanks."

"Want me to keep making you feel better?"

She nearly laughed. Okay, maybe his personality wasn't so horrible. "Please do."

"I, for one, am really happy you're not dating Rupert or The Suit."

"Why?"

"Because if you were, I couldn't do this."

"Do—"

His mouth covered hers before she could say another word. His lips pressed against hers with an urgency that took her breath away. Hunger, desire, need.

His kiss possessed her.

She tasted salt, sweat, and male. An intoxicating, addictive combination she couldn't get enough of.

His razor stubble scratched her face, but she didn't care.

Serena wrapped her arms around his neck and kissed him back. The kiss melded into another and another. She wanted to get closer to him.

As if reading her mind, Kane embraced her. He pressed lightly, placing his hands in a way so he cradled her gently while being cautious of her ribs, drawing her toward him. She went eagerly, wanting more.

She'd never known so much hunger, nor had she ever felt so complete. The emotions contradicted as a battle between mind and body warred inside her.

As his arms tightened around her, she wanted him even closer. His lips lingered, explored, and caressed with such care she could barely stand. But he wanted freedom at any cost.

With his mouth against hers, she felt as if she could soar and never have to land. But he didn't love unconditionally, given what he said about his father. He was oh-so wrong for her.

Nothing made sense. Not Kane kissing her. Not her kissing him back.

With his lips devouring hers, reason and common sense took a back seat. Nothing else mattered. Nothing except more kisses.

She leaned into him, soaking up his strength and his warmth.

Gratitude. That would explain everything.

She kissed Kane back to repay him for all he'd done. But the blood boiling through her veins had nothing to do with thankfulness and everything to do with desire.

Kane kissed her as if she were what kept him alive. He made her feel so special. She didn't deserve it after lying about Rupert, but Kane didn't seem to mind.

He showered her with kiss after kiss after kiss as if this were her reward. She accepted. Gladly.

She'd kissed men before, of course, but all of those seemed like practice to prepare her for this—for the main event.

Everything about his kisses was perfect.

Everything except the man himself.

Serena didn't care.

Oh, she should have cared. And no doubt she would later.

But for now, for this very moment, she wouldn't think so much. She wouldn't analyze. She wouldn't plan.

She would simply…enjoy.

Enjoy the moment.

Enjoy the sensation.

Enjoy Kane.

And she did. They continued to kiss in front of the fire.

Thank goodness he had his arms around her or she might have slipped to the floor. His lips moved from her mouth across her jaw to her ear. He nibbled on her earlobe. Tingles exploded like firecrackers, racing from her ear to her jawline and down her neck, spreading out when they reached her chest.

She gasped. Kane dragged his mouth away.

His breathing was fast and his eyes dark as he stared at her. "I'm sorry. I shouldn't have done that. It won't happen again."

Those were the last words her lips wanted to hear. "But thank you," he added.

Serena hadn't known what to expect, but his saying thanks wasn't it. Granted, a man like Kane probably made out regularly with women. But he didn't even seem to like her much. Not enough to kiss her. Now, he acted as if she'd held open a door for him, not let him plunder and pillage her mouth. "You're welcome?"

He raised a hand to her face and brushed a strand of hair out of her eyes. "Ready?"

Her pounding heart accelerated. "For what?" She sounded as breathless as she felt.

"To get to work."

If she had been a hot air balloon, she would have gone splat against the earth. "Work?"

"We need to unpack, find wood for the stove, a lot of things."

No, she wanted to scream. Her lips felt swollen and bruised. Her insides still tingled. And he wanted to talk about finding wood? Not the kiss?

Serena straightened. If the kiss meant nothing to him, then it meant nothing to her.

And maybe all wedding dresses next season would be hot pink like one of Belle's brides had wanted her gown to be.

"Before we get to work, I have to ask. What was that all about?"

He looked at Serena expectantly.

"The, um, kiss," she clarified.

"An impulse," Kane said with a shrug. "I just wanted to kiss you."

"You just wanted to kiss me?"

"Yeah, you looked like you needed to be kissed. With no boyfriend in the picture, nothing was stopping me."

Okay. Not. "Is this something you do a lot? Kiss women who look like they need a kiss?"

"Not random women on the street. Well, except for this one time in Paris and another in Rome. But generally, with minor exceptions, the answer is no. I don't make a habit of kissing random women. And I only planned to kiss you once."

"What happened?"

"You kissed me back."

Embarrassment burned her cheeks. At least there would be no more kisses. She agreed it shouldn't happen again. Because Serena now knew who she was dealing with.

Forget about being baffled and bewildered any longer. Kane was precisely what she'd known him to be the minute she'd met him. Even though his kiss would have knocked her socks off had she been wearing any, he was the epitome of Mr. Wrong.

In every sense of the word.

Never mind being stranded or the bad weather hanging over them or anything else facing her in the wilderness. The most difficult thing she would have to survive was Kane Wiley. She realized something else, too.

For years, she had blamed her sister for lacking good judgment about men. Touching a finger to her still-throbbing lips, Serena finally understood the appeal of a bad boy. She owed Morgan an apology.

* * *

As Belle stood in her office, Charlie put away his phone. He'd just gotten off a call with the sheriff overseeing the search and rescue effort. "The weather has grounded the air operation, but they plan to get a land search underway once they determine the search grid. I'm flying out there."

Her insides clenched, and she walked to the window. On the street below, life went on. A car honked. People hurried along the sidewalks. A taxi pulled up to the curb, and two well-dressed women exited. But inside her building, everything—except hope and prayers—had stopped.

"Of course you're going," she said.

Belle wouldn't have expected any less from Charlie. She understood he needed to go and be closer to where his son was, but a part of her hated seeing him leave. His presence at the shop this morning had been a blessing to her and the others who worked there.

"Did you speak with Serena's parents?" he asked.

"Yes. They're somewhere in the Himalayas. They decided that by the time they'd make it to an airport, let alone fly back, this will probably all be over with, so they are continuing their trek."

Belle's heart ached for the designer. Pleasing her parents and gaining their approval was important to Serena. She included them in all her triumphs. And they were too busy to come when their daughter needed them most? Belle didn't understand their thought process. "They asked me to pass on information as I hear it. Will you keep me updated?"

Charlie walked to her and linked his fingers with hers. His touch comforted her. His hand felt warm and strong against her skin. "I want you to come with me."

Her heart bumped. "Me?"

"Yes, you." Charlie squeezed her hand. When he let go, she missed the unexpected contact. "Serena might want to see a familiar face when she's found."

"Oh, she definitely needs someone there for her."

"So you'll come?"

Belle wanted to say yes, but she'd heard the anticipation in Charlie's voice, and she couldn't forget the way her heart had reacted when he'd invited her. She wanted to go with him for her own sake as much as Serena's. And that concerned Belle. "Let me talk to Serena's boyfriend first. If he can't go, I will."

GROUP CHAT #4

Elle: *I wasn't able to sleep last night. I keep thinking about Serena.*

Jane: *Same. I hope they're close to finding them.*

Kelsey: *I know, but the weather keeps getting in the way.*

Jane: *That sucks.*

Elle: *What about Serena's parents? Are they flying to Idaho?*

Kelsey: *Belle told me they're on vacation and have decided not to come home. The pilot's father is going to head out there.*

Jane: *What about Rupert?*

Elle: *He must be out of his mind with worry.*

Kelsey: *Belle's going to call Rupert. If he can't go to Idaho, she'll accompany the pilot's father so Serena isn't alone.*

Thirty minutes later...

Kelsey: *I just heard from Belle. She got in touch with Rupert. He's not going to Idaho.*

Jane: *What? Why?*

Elle: *He has to go! Serena's going to need him.*

Kelsey: *Rupert told Belle he broke up with her more than two months ago.*

Jane: *No! She would have told us.*

Elle: *Serena never mentioned it. Never implied it.*

Kelsey: *I know. Belle said no one who works with Serena knew either, so she was keeping the breakup a secret.*

Elle: *But why?*

Kelsey: *She must have her reasons.*

Elle: *We'll just have to ask Serena.*

Jane: *I only hope we get the chance.*

CHAPTER EIGHT

Kane needed to have his head examined.

Stomping around in the snow with flurries falling from the sky didn't make a lot of sense to him. Neither had kissing Serena. He'd only wanted to kiss her once, not a full-on make-out session, but when she'd pressed against him and kissed him back…

At least gathering firewood gave them time and much-needed space away from each other. The cold air didn't hurt, either.

He glanced her way. She was getting a little too far away from him to be safe. "What are you doing?"

Serena waved her hot-pink cell phone in the air with a bare hand. "Seeing if I can get a signal on my cell phone."

City girl. He tried for patience but failed.

"Forget about your phone and put your gloves back on before you get frostbite." He watched her pull his gloves onto her hands. "Look for fallen trees, branches, anything that looks like it might burn."

"Okay."

Nothing was okay.

Kissing Serena was about the dumbest thing he'd done lately. Sure, he'd enjoyed it. One taste and he wanted to kiss her again. But he couldn't let himself get caught up in the moment again. Putting the moves on a woman who couldn't call a cab and was forced to share his bed for survival violated his personal code of conduct.

Kane brushed the snowflakes from his hair with his sock-covered hands. Maybe the rough landing had shaken up more than the plane. His brain wasn't functioning as usual.

He shot a sideward glance at Serena, whose feet sank into the deep snow as she made her way toward him. "Be careful."

"I'm being careful. I know how to take care of myself."

Distance, he reminded himself. "And your dresses."

"You helped with the dresses." She smiled at him. "In fact, you've helped with everything. I'm...not used to that."

Even distance wasn't a shield against her smile. "You don't make it easy."

"I know, but I'm trying to be less..."

"Of a pain in the bottom?"

"Hey." She placed her gloved hands on her coat-covered hips. "You said I had a cute bottom."

"I did. You do. But you can still be a pain."

"I'm trying to be—"

"Not so self-reliant, independent, stubborn?"

Her mouth quirked. "I was going to say more receptive."

To his help? To his kisses? To him?

Only the first mattered. He focused on a large branch lying in the snow. "That would make things easier."

He looked at her bright blue eyes and flushed cheeks.

Then again, maybe not.

Kane dragged the branch to the end of the trail leading to the cabin. Serena added a smaller branch of her own.

"I'm not used to admitting I can't handle everything myself," she said quietly.

"You don't have to." She'd shown glimpses of vulnerability, but now, she didn't seem so afraid to let him know what she was feeling. "Just don't pretend you can."

"I won't."

Kane might have found her emotional honesty attractive on one level, but it was equally inconvenient on several others. Her being vulnerable with him did not mean he would be the same to her. He was not going there. He didn't open himself up to anybody.

And that was the way he was keeping it.

* * *

On board a plane heading for Idaho, Belle stared out the window. The sight of the landscape below, the acres of green fields giving way to tree-covered mountainsides, reminded her of Serena and Kane lost somewhere in the wilderness. Belle closed her eyes. She needed time to regroup and put her game face on, as Calista, their resident poker expert, called it.

Belle hated leaving Boston when everyone who worked in her building was distraught, but at least they had each other. Serena needed someone to be there for her. Still, a few hours ago, the tears had fallen like raindrops during a Georgia thunderstorm. The hugs and goodbyes had mingled with their hopes and fears. Belle had canceled appointments and put her business on hold. That was the right thing to do until she returned to Boston with Serena.

If she returned with Serena…

Belle blew out a puff of air.

"Hang in there." Charlie sat in the aisle seat next to her. "We can't give up hope." The compassion in his voice tugged on Belle's heartstrings.

"I'm trying. But not knowing anything is hard. A part of me fears what we might find when we get there."

"Sometimes not knowing is better," Charlie admitted. "I remember…"

"What?" She leaned toward him. "Tell me, please."

"Three years ago, I got a phone call from Kane telling me his mother, my wife, had suffered a heart attack. He asked me to meet him at the hospital. What he didn't tell me was that the massive coronary had killed her."

"Oh, Charlie." Memories of losing her husband, tucked deep in her heart, floated to the surface. She remembered the emotions as if they were brand new and raw, not nine years old. Disbelief, shock, and loneliness had rooted themselves in her heart, only to be somewhat pruned with the passage of time. Belle covered Charlie's hand with her own. "That must have been horrible."

"Not at first. I didn't know," he said. "As I drove to the hospital, I worried she might need surgery. That scared me, but the idea of her dying? My mind wouldn't let me go there, or I would have fallen apart."

Belle gave his hand a gentle squeeze. "When my husband, Matthew, got sick, I knew it was serious. He was older than me, but I believed with all my heart he would recover. I don't know how I could have given him the support, the care he'd needed, if I'd thought he was leaving me."

"I had worked everything out in my head by the time I arrived at the hospital. How she would recover, what needed to be done, and then Kane told me and…"

"Your world fell apart."

Charlie nodded.

"Mine, too," she said. "At first, you have so much to take care of—all the paperwork, the people around you. I felt as if I was living in a fog."

"But the work ends, the people go away, and the cloud of shock lifts. And you're left…"

"With nothing." Belle felt a connection, a new bond growing between her and Charlie. "And if you're like me, you're utterly lost, don't know what to do, and end up making some really bad decisions."

Surprise filled his eyes. "I thought I was the only one who did that."

"Oh, darlin', I wish that was the case because I made some doozies. A stuffed Thanksgiving turkey had more sense than I did during those first two years."

He laughed. So did Belle.

"I'm happy you're with me." His brown eyes darkened to the color of espresso. "No matter what we find out, we'll make it through."

She nodded.

"We'll keep each other from making any doozy mistakes, too," he added. "That's what friends are for."

Friends.

When they'd left Boston, Belle had thought she only wanted friendship from Charlie. But as she sat here with her hand on top of his and talked with him this way, the word didn't seem nearly enough for her.

Must be the situation, she rationalized. The heightened emotions. The terrifying unknowns. Nothing else made sense.

"Do we have a deal, Belle?"

She pulled her hand from the top of his to shake on his words. "Deal, darlin'."

* * *

That evening in the cabin, Kane sat across from Serena. She stared at the remnants of their dinner—canned stew, crackers, and dried fruit—littering the table. Not exactly gourmet fare.

"Thanks for cooking dinner tonight," he said. "The meal hit the spot after gathering all that wood."

She placed the wrappers from the crackers on her plate. "That wasn't cooking. I wish the biscuits had turned out."

"Hey, I'm impressed you even attempted biscuits." He leaned back in his chair. "How are your ribs? Sore?"

"A little."

The rest of Serena's muscles ached, especially her back. Pilates and running, her normal workouts, couldn't compare to gathering firewood in the falling snow.

What she wouldn't give for a massage.

She stretched, happy she'd changed out of her skirt and sweater into her flannel pajama bottoms and a turtleneck. It was so nice to be in her own clothes, and she was grateful that Kane had thought of her when he went to the plane. So long as she didn't have to make a late-night run to the outhouse, she'd stay comfy and warm.

Serena glanced around the small cabin, surprisingly content. The crackling wood in the stove kept the temperature comfortable. The propane lighting provided a soft glow. And her companion...

"Dessert?" Kane asked.

She would have rather had that massage. But dessert was a safer bet than Kane's soothing hands making her aching body feel better. "Let me clean up first."

"No, dessert comes first. Always."

As he rummaged through the food, she studied him. Kane was a contradiction. One minute gruff, the next giving. Serena appreciated his softer, gentler side. To be honest, she kind of liked being taken care of. Not that she would ever tell him that. Or anybody, for that matter.

She'd had to be dependable and self-reliant for so long. She'd dressed to glossy perfection and portrayed the image of a successful wedding dress designer with practiced flair and finesse. But she was out of her element now and needing to rely on Kane, something she'd never had to do. The competency she prided herself on was limited to the scope of her known world, and that was a sobering thought.

But in a way, this experience was eye opening. Rupert might have been harsh, but he was right. Her need to have everything so well in hand didn't leave room for a true partnership. That was something she needed to examine once she got home.

Out there in the mountains, in this cozy little cabin with Kane, however, she could just be herself. She could forget about everyone else's expectations and relax. She could finally be…free.

No wonder Kane wanted freedom. It felt good.

He extended his arm and offered her a handful of truffles. "Here you go."

She plucked a heart-shaped chocolate wrapped in cellophane and tied with a lavender ribbon from his hand. "Thanks."

"Just one?"

"This will hit the spot."

"Chocolate always does."

"A man after my own heart." Serena felt his gaze on her. "What?"

"I thought you were a no-chocolate girl."

She unwrapped the piece. "Why?"

"At the bridal show, you didn't eat any."

"Those are considered merchandise and only for show attendees."

"But now that the show is over..."

"We can have as many as we want. They won't be reused."

He half laughed. "I figured you were a perpetual dieter who scorned sweets."

"Are you kidding?" She raised the truffle to her nose and sniffed. Heavenly. "I eat wedding cake samples all the time. Chocolate is my favorite." Serena bit into the crisp dark chocolate shell, and the taste exploded in her mouth. Sweet and rich, with a hint of bitterness. The creamy inside melted on her tongue. "Mmm."

"That good?"

Nodding, she savored the texture as she took another bite. Oh-so yummy but addictive. A little like a kiss from Kane; you wanted more than one taste. But like the handful of truffles he offered her, one was more than enough. Any more wouldn't be wise.

When she was finished, a faint sugary scent remained on her fingertips. At least Kane's kiss hadn't left that on her lips. Serena looked across the table at him. "Aren't you having one?"

"I had two." A devilish grin appeared. "You were too busy enjoying yours to notice."

"Sorry."

"Don't be. I like a woman who can appreciate what's good for her."

"I consider myself a chocolate connoisseur."

"And how do you become a chocolate connoisseur?"

She smiled. "By eating lots and lots of chocolate."

"Then I must be a connoisseur, too." He picked up the carafe he'd brought from the plane and filled their glasses with water he'd melted from the snow. "Make sure you drink all of it. You don't want to get dehydrated."

Serena sipped the warm water, a comforting silence settling between them. They were more like a couple on vacation in a mountain cabin than two strangers stranded together in the wilderness.

She watched him as he drank from a mug, mesmerized, wishing his lips were touching hers instead. Her cup slipped from her right hand, but she caught it with her left, only spilling a few drops.

Uh-oh. If she wasn't careful, she could be the one crashing to the floor. Serena rose and cleared the table.

"You like playing house, don't you?" Kane asked.

She carried the plates and glanced his way, suddenly cautious. "I don't play house."

"Never?"

"Never," she admitted, thinking about Morgan. "I've seen what can go wrong when you play."

"You surprise me, Blondie."

"What do you mean?"

"Underneath all that shine and glamour, you're an old-fashioned girl. Cleaning the cabin. Cooking dinner. Now, the dishes."

Old-fashioned? Serena tried to decide whether his comment offended her. "It's not old-fashioned to want a tidy living space. I grew up doing chores."

"I never did chores." Kane stood. "My mom or the housekeeper did everything."

Serena had been the one to do everything. She'd done her own chores—her sister's, too. Anything she could to make things…perfect.

He took the dishes from her hands. "I've got these."

"I don't mind," she said automatically, reaching for the stack.

But he wouldn't let go. "I do."

The two held on to the plates as if they were made of fine porcelain, not plastic.

"What are you doing, Blondie?" Kane asked finally. "Trying to earn a gold star on your chore chart?"

Serena blushed. How could he know her so well? "Well, I always did get a lot of gold stars."

"Such a good girl." His lips curved in a teasing, charming, coaxing smile. "Let me do the dishes tonight."

Reluctantly, she let go. "Then what will I do?"

"To earn those gold stars?" His eyes gleamed. "I'm sure we can think of something."

* * *

After he cleaned the dishes, Kane stoked the fire. Now, all he needed to do was crawl into bed. Strike that. Bed brought up the image of making out with the sexy blonde who kissed like a dream. Scowling, he rubbed the back of his neck.

"Are you all right?" Serena sat at the table. "You look tense."

He fought the urge to laugh. "I'm fine."

Her pretty blue eyes widened in sympathy. "It's the bed. It's not big enough for two."

Unless they slept stacked like firewood. And then Kane could guarantee they'd get no sleep at all.

"The bed's fine," he said. "I just need—"

You.

"A pillow," he finished, not knowing what else to say without giving himself away.

Serena perked up. She pulled one of her boxes toward her and searched through it until she pulled out a plump purple velvet square. "Aha. One pillow."

Kane raised his eyebrows. "That wasn't in the booth at the show."

"I know. I didn't use it because I couldn't find the slipper."

Kane had no idea what she was talking about. "What slipper?"

"The glass slipper. Cinderella's slipper?"

He continued to stare at her.

She sighed. "You know. Fairy Godmother, Prince Charming, stroke of midnight, happily ever after?"

He shook his head. "Ah, the slipper. I don't believe in that stuff."

"Stuff?"

"Fairy tales and happy endings."

"Why not?"

Thinking about his father and his ex-stepmother left a bitter taste in Kane's mouth. "Happy endings aren't possible because love is transitory. It doesn't last. It can't. As soon as a so-called love is gone, the other person is on to the next one."

A beat passed. And another.

The only sounds were the crackling of the fire in the stove and their breathing.

"It isn't always like that," she said.

This conversation made him...weary. He headed toward the bed. Maybe she would get the clue he didn't want to talk about this.

"I believe fairy-tale endings exist. I know it doesn't happen for everyone. My sister is a prime example, but that's because she was with the wrong guy. I know of others who have stood by their significant other through good and bad," she continued, her words full of longing. "Disappointment or failure, it doesn't matter because even when things are at their darkest, no matter what horrible things might happen, their love will remain strong and solid. Forever."

He forced himself not to laugh. "You want that?"

"Yes, and I intend to have it. Someday," she added as if the timing were an afterthought.

He was more moved—and more shaken—than he wanted to admit. "You believe that if you want to."

"What do you believe?" she asked softly.

Looking into her blue eyes, Kane wanted to believe in *her.*

And that scared him even more than her talk about forever.

He deflected her question with a smile. "I believe in the benefits of a good night's sleep. Toss that pillow over here, and let's get some shut-eye."

* * *

The following day passed slowly. Snow continued to fall, keeping them trapped inside the cabin. Serena wanted to make use of the time, so she sketched new dress design ideas while Kane worked on an electric box from the plane. By the time evening came and dinner was over, she was ready to do something to work off some energy and take her mind off their plight. Anything.

She glanced at Kane while he sat at the table. Okay, not anything.

Serena paced the small confines of the cabin. The smell from the woodstove seemed to intensify, and she longed to feel a cool breeze on her face. What she wouldn't have given to smell the ocean or cocoa butter, anything tropical.

She'd counted the mice scurrying across the floor—three—and wondered if naming them would be a good idea. That would keep her occupied, which would be a good thing. Boredom might lead her and Kane to do something they shouldn't do to, well, keep themselves busy.

Her hand rose to her lips, and she lowered it.

Serena couldn't think about him that way.

No more kisses.

Walking away from his father the way he had showed her that he didn't believe in unconditional love. Not that it mattered to her what he believed. They were a step above strangers, mere acquaintances trapped together by an unusual circumstance. At that thought, a flicker of disappointment shot through her.

"Bored?" he asked.

She shrugged. "A little."

"Cabin fever is no fun."

It was better than another kind of fever, like baby fever. She gulped. "I'm sure we can think of something to do."

She bet they could. That was what worried her.

Outside, a wolf howled somewhere in the distance. She shivered.

Think. Think. Think.

"I have a game for couples to get to know each other better somewhere," she suggested. "Though we're not a couple."

"No, but we are sleeping together."

Serena glared at him.

He laughed. "Don't worry. You're still the kind of girl a guy would want to take home to meet the parents. My father thinks you're great."

She smiled. "Your dad is so sweet."

"He has his moments." Kane got this faraway look in his eyes when he talked about Charlie that suggested he wasn't as indifferent to his dad as he pretended.

The wolf howled again, the lonely cry cutting through the cold night air.

"What about your mom?" she asked, intrigued enough to want to know more about Kane.

"If my mom were still alive, she would like you." Kane's voice was full of warmth.

Serena sat across from him. "What was she like?"

"She was the best and had so much love to give." A soft smile formed on his lips. "The two of you...you have a lot in common. She was into clothes, loved to

146

sew, and subscribed to a stack of fashion magazines. My mom would have talked your ear off about what you do, and she would have invited you to go shopping." Kane's tone rang with a deep love for his mother.

His words wrapped around Serena like an old quilt, comfy and warm and stitched with affection. "She sounds wonderful."

"She was."

The two simple words spoke volumes when coupled with the emotion—the love—in his eyes. And that was when Serena realized Kane Wiley wasn't totally the loner or the free spirit he claimed to be. She had seen his passion with his flying and experienced it with his kiss. She'd also realized that he felt loss deeply. Buried inside had to be a man with a streak of romance, longing for commitment. If only she could get to see that side of him, that would give her a sense of hope that Mr. Right might actually be closer than she thought...

"Tell me what your parents would think if you brought me home to meet them," he said, surprising her.

"They would not like you at all."

He laughed.

Oh no. Had she said that out loud? Her cheeks burned. "It's just that my parents have a well-defined view of who would make an acceptable...partner for their daughters. My mother and father are overachievers. That's what they raised my sister, Morgan, and me to be."

"Looks like they succeeded."

With me, at least. "They want us to be happy."

"Happiness to them is having you marry some guy in a suit with a solid background, a stable job, and a good income with the potential for more so you will have whatever you want or need."

He'd nailed it. "Pretty much."

"You want the same thing?"

His words hung in the air as if they floated in front of her like special effects in a movie. *You want the same thing?* She thought about what she wanted most of all. She wanted her plans to be realized. She wanted to make people happy. She wanted…

An answer formed deep inside her and burst to the surface. "I want true love."

"Ah, the fairy tale again." He studied her, but his gaze was serious with no hint of humor. "You've got everything figured out."

She raised her chin. "I've got a plan."

"Let's hear it."

That surprised her. "Really?"

"I wouldn't ask if I didn't want to know."

This would at least give them something to discuss, a topic that would show how different they were. "Well, once I find Mr. Right, we date for a year, are engaged for a year, get married, buy a house, wait another year before we get pregnant, and then we have a baby."

Kane laughed. "I don't know whether to be impressed at you knowing what you want or worried for the poor guy you choose."

Her cheeks felt warm once again. She didn't remember blushing this much around Rupert. "I'm a planner."

"Nothing wrong with that, except sometimes plans don't work out the way you think they will."

"Tell me about it." Serena sighed. Kane was so easy to talk to. She'd been more upfront and honest with him, whom she'd known—and fought with—for only a couple of days, than with the women she'd known since she was eighteen and those she'd worked with for years. "I'm missing the most important thing in my plan. Mr. Right."

"Hey." He reached across the table and touched the corner of her mouth with his fingertip. "Smile, Blondie. He's out there."

"You think?" She cringed at the insecurity in those two words.

"I know," Kane reassured. "Think positively."

She felt anything but positive. "He's out there. Somewhere."

"Absolutely. You'll find him."

Serena nodded once and stared at the table.

"Look." He lifted her chin with his finger. "I'm about as far away from Mr. Right as you would want, but if you'd like, I could be your Mr. Right Now."

CHAPTER NINE

*M*r. *Right Now.*

Kane shook his head in self-disgust. What was he thinking?

As if Miss Seeking Happily Ever After Tied Up In A Neat Little Bow would settle for a torrid three-day-or-less fling with a no-strings flyboy.

Not that he didn't like the idea. He liked it a lot. He liked her a lot.

Which was part of the problem.

She'd have been a lot easier to resist if she were the spoiled ice princess he'd pegged her as at their first meeting.

The wolf howled again. Louder this time. Closer.

Serena's forehead wrinkled. Her mouth tightened.

Uh-oh. He rose from the table and snuck a peek out of the window. The darkness prevented him from seeing anything outside. "The howl is likely because of a dog barking somewhere. The wolf won't bother us."

Or shouldn't under normal circumstances. But with their luck…

The howl turned into howls.

Right on cue. Kane shook his head, but he shouldn't have been surprised.

Turning slightly, Serena craned her neck to peer at the door. "That sounds like more than one wolf."

"Probably a family," he said nonchalantly, wanting to take away the wariness in her voice. "A dad, mom, pups."

"You mean a pack."

The continued howling intensified. A shuffling sounded outside. Something scratched at the door.

Tension filled the cabin. The lighting seemed to dim. Serena's lower lip quivered. Not a lot, but enough so he noticed. She looked stiff, tight, scared. Maybe he'd mistaken fear for tension.

Kane didn't feel like smiling now but forced one anyway. "We're inside. They're outside. No worries."

"No worries," Serena repeated quietly but kept her head turned and her eyes focused on the door.

He didn't blame her, and he realized how much safer they were in this cabin than if they'd been stuck in the plane with wolves surrounding them. But if she kept that position for any length of time, she would add a cramped neck to her injuries.

Not on my watch.

Kane carried his chair over and wedged the top under the door handle. "Wolves usually stay away from humans. I've never known a wolf to open a door, but in case these Idaho ones know any special tricks, the chair will add a little insurance."

As she turned to face him, her shoulders relaxed. "Thanks."

He blew out a puff of air. Now what? "So…"

"So what does a Mr. Right Now do?"

Man, Kane thought he'd gotten away with that one scot-free. He was trying to resist temptation, but if temptation—or Serena—threw itself in his lap… "Whatever you want him to do."

The howling continued, but Serena didn't glance at the door. She stood instead. With a mix of anticipation and alarm, her gaze met his. "Would you hold me?"

In a New York minute.

Her vulnerable expression smacked him right in the gut. He sat on Serena chair and pulled her onto his lap. "How's this?"

"Nice."

Nice didn't begin to describe how good holding her on his lap felt. More like perfect.

Wolves continued to howl outside. Wind blew through the trees and rattled the windows. Wood burned in the stove, crackling and popping, with the now familiar scent of smoke wafting in the air.

Nothing else existed. Nothing else mattered.

He wrapped his arms around her. Soft and warm and all his. Well, for as long as she allowed.

"Thank you," she murmured.

He should have been thanking her. And the wolves. "No problem."

It wasn't.

Not now.

Ask him again in a few minutes.

"It's probably silly to be frightened of a few overgrown dogs," she said. "But the wolves were the final straw after everything that's happened. I'm not very good at this adventure stuff."

He ran his finger along her jaw to her chin. Soft, with a determined edge. Like the woman herself. "Being out here alone is nothing like living in Boston."

She smiled. "But I'm not alone. I have you."

Kane swallowed. "For now."

He wasn't in this for the long haul. One of them had to remember that.

She leaned back, giving him the chance to nuzzle his nose against her hair. The scent no longer smelled like strawberries, sweet and fresh and juicy, but she must have used something in her bag. Her smell reminded him of spring—flowers blooming and sunny days—not a day in early November with drifting snow outside as far as the eye could see. He took another sniff. Her lotion? Or just Serena?

The answer didn't matter.

Not with her on his lap, in his arms, snuggling against him as if she belonged there. His blood boiled, pounding through his veins. He needed to think cool thoughts. Arctic thoughts might work best.

"You want to know something?" Serena asked.

Anything to stop thinking about her and the way she smelled. "What?"

"Even though I feel out of sorts tonight, I'd rather be here than in Boston."

Her words shot straight to his heart, crashing through his defenses with their sincerity. "Me, too."

If Kane were smart, he would end this right now. The situation had *bad news* written all over it. She wasn't looking for something temporary. He wasn't looking for something permanent. Someone would get hurt.

No, he would make sure that didn't happen.

He respected Serena too much to hurt her by taking advantage of her trust and the situation.

All Kane wanted to do was hold her. Well, not all. But it would do. It had to.

He pulled her closer, careful of her ribs, mindful of where he placed his hands. Her heartbeat drummed against him, the increasing tempo matching his own.

Another noise sounded outside the door. Wind? Wolf? Hard to tell.

Serena turned her face right next to his. Her warm breath fanned his cheek. Big blue eyes stared deep into his, probing and searching.

Attraction buzzed between them. The thrum of awareness grew.

Kane's self-control slipped a notch. Okay, two.

She'd asked him to hold her. She wanted comfort, but the flash of desire in her eyes and her parted lips told him she also wanted…

"Kiss me," she whispered. "Please."

She wouldn't have to ask twice.

Brushing his lips over hers, Kane wanted to soothe her. Calm and reassure her, too. He wanted his kiss to make her feel special, that she was cherished and adored. The way a woman should always feel.

This kiss was different, sweeter and softer than the ones yesterday, but just as good. With each passing moment, he struggled to keep the kiss gentle and not allow his growing desire to take over. Hard to do when she was in his arms and kissing him back.

Talk about heaven on earth.

It couldn't get much better than this.

She leaned into the kiss, pressing her lips harder against his.

So much for tenderness.

His blood pressure spiraled. Logical thought disappeared. Common sense fled.

There was only here and now.

Only Serena.

The realization should have bothered him more than it did, but Kane didn't care. Right now, this…she…was all that mattered. He ran his hands through her hair, the short strands sifting through his fingers.

Pulling her closer, he deepened the kiss. She tasted like chocolate. Expensive and rich and addictive. He wanted another taste. And another.

Her fingertips ran along the muscles on his back, rubbing, kneading, exploring. Her eagerness pleased him. Turned him on. Made him want more.

Want her.

Want all…

Whoa. This was getting out of control. Who was he kidding? The situation was reaching the breaking point.

Kane had to stop kissing her. Now.

Before the kisses turned into something more. He couldn't do that to Serena, even if she was the one who had asked for the kiss. She needed more than he was willing to give her. She wanted a man who would commit. Just like Amber and every other woman he'd known. He wasn't that man.

He kissed Serena, soaking up the taste of her for one last time, then pulled away. Her breathing ragged, she looked at him with those big eyes, eyes clouded with desire for him, and full lips, bruised and swollen from kissing him. He'd never seen a woman look sexier or more beautiful.

Kane struggled to breathe.

"Wow." She scooted off his lap and stood next to the table. "I'm not sure what to say."

"Thank you would suffice."

She smiled shyly. "Thank you."

"Anytime. I mean, if you want something or need…"

"I know what you mean, Kane."

That made one of them, because he hadn't a clue.

"What now?" Serena asked.

Oh, he had many ideas, but none would be good for her. Or, come to think of it, him. "Sleep."

"Sleep?" She sounded a little confused.

That made two of them.

Why did she have to be so sweet, so pretty, so sexy? Why did she want to find true love? Why couldn't they…

"Maybe I should sleep on the floor," he said. "On blankets."

"You want to sleep on the floor?" she asked, her voice as soft as a snowflake. "Is that really what you want to do?"

Forget about what he wanted to do. That would only make things worse. "It's probably a good idea tonight. Taking this physical stuff any further—"

"Wouldn't be smart," she finished for him. "But I hate for you to sleep on the floor. What if we just agreed to be on our best behavior, a gentleman and a gentlewoman, and make sure nothing else happened?"

"Would you feel comfortable enough with that?"

She nodded. "I trust you, Kane."

Her words pierced his heart like an arrow shot at the bull's-eye. Direct hit.

He nearly staggered back a step. Well, he would have if he'd been standing.

But his heart didn't hurt. It wanted…more.

That only meant one thing. Serena was getting too close. Kane knew exactly what he had to do—or, rather, what he couldn't do. No more cuddling, no more kisses, and no more Mr. Right Now.

Tempted or not, his heart was off-limits. And he wasn't about to change.

* * *

"We have pinpointed a possible location," the on-scene incident commander Logan Michaels explained to Charlie and Belle at a mobile command post in Clearwater National Forest. He pointed at a large topographical map with red marks and circles drawn on it. "The weather has the air search grounded again, but members of a search and rescue team are riding to Gold Meadows on horseback. In a situation like this, we put calls out for assistance. County and state lines don't matter much. We've got a unit from Missoula, Montana, waiting to assist with the evacuation and another group on standby."

Excitement surged through Belle. "Wonderful news to start the day."

"It is," Charlie said. "Worthy of a hug."

She nodded and hugged him. His arms wrapped around her, and heat rushed up her cheeks. She hadn't dated since Matthew's death, so the tingles in her stomach surprised her. Still, they felt good. A little strange but right.

She enjoyed having someone to lean on after having been on her own for so long.

Charlie released her. His eye-reaching grin filled Belle with surprising joy.

"How did you pinpoint them?" he asked.

"Cell phone technology," Logan said. "A local cellular company found pings from one of the phones."

Belle mouthed a silent prayer. "It's amazing that one of them still has power after all this time. Though Serena carries a charging pack."

Charlie looked at her. His mouth was tight. His jaw set.

Belle didn't know him well, but she knew enough about him to know the question he wanted answered. A question he couldn't ask himself. "Do you know whose cell phone had been turned on? Kane's or Serena's?"

"Serena's," Logan answered.

A shadow crossed Charlie's face.

Belle reached for him, linking her hand with his. "That doesn't mean—"

"I know."

"Kane's could be out of power," she said. "We don't know enough to make any assumptions."

"Belle is correct, Charlie," Logan said. "Your concern is understandable, given the circumstances, but there are so many factors we just don't know. What you can count on is the experience and expertise of the SAR unit out there searching for Kane and Serena."

"SAR?" Belle asked.

"Search and rescue," Logan explained. "You won't find a better group of men and women. One of the best SAR experts in the country is out there, too. Jake Porter. He's with Oregon Mountain Search and Rescue and was training our unit this past weekend. When the call came in on Sunday, he decided to stay on and join the team in the field."

Belle forced a smile. "Well, you can't ask for more than that, can you, darlin'?"

The strain on Charlie's face eased. "I guess you can't. We appreciate your efforts, Logan. And everyone else out there in the cold, snowy weather looking for Kane and Serena."

"You're welcome." Logan pointed at a map. "Just so you know, Gold Meadows has been used in the past as a helicopter landing site while fighting forest fires. There's also a small cabin there with provisions, light, and heat."

"More good news." Belle smiled, hoping for the best.

"It could be. I'll let you know when I hear more news," Logan said. "I also want to let you know the media has picked up the story. You may be asked for a statement. It's your choice if you talk to them or not. The sheriff's office has a public relations liaison who'll work with you."

"Thank you," Belle and Charlie spoke at the same time.

His gaze caught hers. His brown eyes seemed to see straight to her heart. Warmth flooded through her like a sip of hot cocoa with a dash of peppermint schnapps mixed in. The reaction was unexpected but not unwelcome.

The realization set off about a zillion warning bells in her head. She'd had her chance at the love of a lifetime with her beloved Matthew. She didn't want a boyfriend, let alone something serious.

Still, Belle found herself sneaking another peek at the handsome and charming Charlie.

GROUP CHAT #5

Kelsey: *I just heard from Belle! They've picked up a signal from Serena's cell phone! The area where the plane went down has a cabin, so if they found that, they'll have shelter and food. The biggest issue right now is the weather. That's slowing the search.*

Jane: *Oh! I hope they're in the cabin right now waiting out the weather.*

Elle: *Me, too! I keep waiting for Serena to jump on the chat and say she's fine.*

Jane: *I want that more than anything.*

Kelsey: *Same, but we'll just have to be patient.*

Elle: *We have been, and that's not one of my strong points, but whatever we're feeling, I'm sure it's worse for Serena and the pilot.*

Jane: *I just hope they're not injured.*

Kelsey: *As soon as I hear more, I'll let you know!*

CHAPTER TEN

The following morning, Serena woke feeling rested and warm as if she were waking in her own bed at home, not in a rustic little cabin in the snow-covered woods. Kane lay with his chest against her back, his arm draped over her hip, and his legs entwined with hers.

His breath caressed her neck. The warm puffs comforted her the same way his snores had during the night.

She'd held up her end of the bargain, and so had he. Kane had been the perfect gentleman as promised. Just like she had known he would be. But that hadn't made things any easier.

She touched her lips. Slightly swollen as if she'd used a plumping lipstick. But these lips were strictly the result of Kane, not some cosmetic recipe.

"Kiss me, please."

Serena couldn't believe she'd said those words. She wished she could blame her lapse in judgment on fear of the wolves and a sudden realization they were truly lost, but she knew better. Being held had eased her worry but ignited a spark. One that didn't want to be doused.

She'd wanted to be kissed. She'd needed to be kissed.

By him.

Only him.

Kane had delivered. His kisses made her feel safe and accepted. He made her feel beautiful without her usual gloss of manners and accomplishments, without the armor of designer clothing, without styling gel and concealer. Sexy. Herself.

She could be herself, and that was enough. Freeing.

Serena couldn't see him, but her heart filled with satisfaction.

Uh-oh. She couldn't forget that this wasn't real. Kane had said they were just playing house—make that cabin—and for now, she would enjoy it despite the pack of wolves and an occasional mouse scampering across the floor. What had happened there never would have happened in Boston.

It couldn't.

Still, the experience only reaffirmed what she wanted in life. Serena was tired of living to meet other people's expectations and demands. She loved her parents, but she'd been trying too hard to live up to what they wanted from her. No, she didn't need to rebel as Morgan had, but she needed to follow her dreams. Her heart.

She wanted a man who would love her for herself. Without strings. Without conditions. She wanted to find what she'd found temporarily in Kane's arms.

If only it could be him…

No. She couldn't allow herself to even daydream about that. Even if she wanted to live for herself now, she wanted that forever kind of love. Something he was clear he didn't want. That was why Kane Wiley could never be her Mr. Right. He'd admitted that himself.

But still, her heart wanted him.

Not going to happen.

All Serena had to do was push emotion aside and look at the situation logically. Look at Kane that way, too. Mentally, she composed a list of everything wrong with him.

1. Does not love unconditionally

2. Cannot forgive

3. No longer believes in happily ever after

4. Values freedom more than anything, including relationships

5. Kisses so well that reasons 1–4 don't matter

She groaned.

Not a problem. Despite number five, she had learned from Morgan's mistakes and would not repeat them.

Serena pulled her leg away from his and crawled off the bed quietly. The wood floor was cold beneath her sock-covered feet. She padded to the window. No sign of any wolves, but the snow continued to fall.

Disappointment settled in the bottom of her gut. More snow meant another day and night in the cabin. And at least another twenty-four tempting hours with Kane.

Don't think about that.

Instead, Serena got busy. She added wood to the stove to keep the cabin warm, dressed in her heaviest skirt, and reminded herself to always pack warm clothes when traveling from now on. She needed to use the outhouse but hesitated at the door.

What if the wolves were still out there? She opened the door slowly. Pawprints were everywhere.

"Going somewhere, Blondie?"

The rich sound of his voice sent the butterflies in her stomach fluttering. Those needed to stop right now. "I was seeing if the wolves were still there."

"Are they?"

Feeling tongue-tied, she shrugged.

What was going on? She was Serena James, the hottest new name in wedding dress design. She had her own studio and her own condo. She always knew the right thing to say, whether talking with a friend or giving a sound bite. She was capable, successful, and reliable. But Kane made her feel like she was back in middle school, thin and awkward-looking, standing against the gym wall by herself, waiting to be asked to dance.

"Want to wear a pair of my pants so you'll be warmer?" he asked.

"I don't think they'd fit, but if they did, I'd have to stop eating."

A corner of his mouth turned up. "I'm sure, with your vast fashion expertise, you could figure out a way to keep my pants on you."

"Thanks, but this skirt is wool." She remembered how intimate wearing his shirt the first night had felt. His pants would be worse. No more intimacy allowed!

"Suit yourself." He grabbed a pair of jeans from his bag. "I'm going to change clothes. Then I'll make sure there aren't any more four-footed visitors hanging around outside."

Serena glanced out of the window at the falling snow. She felt as if she were falling, too, and didn't like it one bit. The only way to get what she wanted was to be in control. She'd figured that out years ago.

As the teeth of a zipper being undone filled the quiet cabin, a flare of heat burst through her, and she grimaced at her reaction. So much for self-control.

She didn't understand why Kane had such an effect on her, but somehow, she had to learn how to control her reactions. No way would she do anything she might regret with Mr. Wrong.

Even if she might like it.

* * *

During breakfast, Kane kept the topics of conversation light—weather, food, and sports teams. Anything to distance himself from Serena, because the first thing he'd wanted to do when he woke up and saw her was kiss her good morning. So much for off-limits.

Time to get serious.

"I'm going to hike to the plane," he said into the silence after they'd washed the dishes.

"I'll come with you."

"No." The word came out harsher than he had intended. "Stay here and doodle in your book."

"Do you mean this book?" She pulled a notebook out of her bag. "This is a sketch pad. I use it to come up with design ideas."

"Stay here and work." He ignored the hurt in her eyes because he couldn't afford to care. "It's better than you getting cold."

"I don't faint in the cold."

A knock sounded on the door.

Serena looked at him.

Another knock.

"I don't think it's the wolves." He sprang out of his chair and opened the door. Five people stood outside. The first four wore matching green jackets. The fifth, hanging back, wore a red-and-black jacket. Kane smiled. "We're so glad to see you."

"I'm Ray Massey," the first in green, a man in his early forties, said. "With the Idaho County Sheriff's Posse."

"Kane Wiley." He motioned behind him. "This is Serena James. Come in."

The team entered the cabin, crowding the small space even more.

"Are either of you injured?" Ray asked.

"Serena has a cut on her head. Her ribs and stomach are bruised."

"We're Wilderness First Responders, and a couple of us are EMTs, too," Ray said to her. "Can we examine you?"

"That's fine," she said.

"Freeman and Porter," Ray ordered.

Freeman wore a heavy green jacket with the words *Sheriff's Posse* written in black on the back. Porter wore a black-and-red jacket with the initials *OMSAR* written in white on the front and *Rescue* on the sleeves.

"Nice setup. Warm. Dry." Ray looked around. "Good job."

"Great job getting to us," Kane said. "How'd you find us?"

"Cell phone pings."

Serena's little pink phone. He'd told her to put the silly thing away. Good thing she hadn't listened to him. He admired her resourcefulness and stubbornness but felt like an idiot for not pulling out his cell phone.

Kane looked over at her, feeling a burst of protectiveness when he saw the two men examining her bare stomach. The one in green knelt in front of her while the one in red and black stood.

"Don't worry," Freeman said to Serena. "I've done this before."

"On a dummy," one of his team members teased.

"Nah, don't you remember?" another team member said. "He got his junior certification last week."

Serena laughed, the tension evaporating from her shoulders.

"You're in good hands, miss," Ray said. "Freeman's new at this, but Porter is from Oregon Mountain Search and Rescue. He knows what he's doing."

She looked up at Porter. "I've seen those mountain rescues in Oregon on the news. I'm sure you know what to do."

"Hey," Freeman said. "We have mountains in Idaho, too."

Porter winked. "You've got foothills here, kid."

All three laughed.

Serena caught Kane staring at her. "What?"

He took a deep breath. It didn't stop the strange feeling in his stomach. "Good job, Blondie. You and that hot-pink phone of yours got us rescued."

"Really?"

Ray nodded. "The cell phone company used your pings to determine your location."

"That's great." Her eyes twinkled. "Guess I contributed something to this adventure after all."

"You contributed a lot more than that, Serena."

As a thousand-watt smile lit up her face, Kane's mouth went dry. And that was when he knew. Oh, maybe he'd already figured it out, but he hadn't admitted it to himself earlier. Now, he had no doubt. She'd gotten under his skin somehow and wormed her way into his heart.

Good thing they were getting out of here.

"Her head is healing nicely with the two butterfly bandages. No sign of infection. No evidence of a concussion," Freeman reported to Ray. "Her ribs are sore. She is likely only bruised but should have an X-ray to rule out a fracture. She can make it out on her own. No need to strap her into a litter."

"Porter?" Ray asked. "How'd the newbie do?"

"The newbie did fine," Porter said. "Good assessment, kid."

"We'll call this in to let people know we found you two and report your condition. Then we'll get out of here before the weather intensifies and prevents travel." Ray clapped his hands. "We've got clothes for you to change into. We may have to do something about your boots, though, miss. Those heels might cause some problems."

"You'd be surprised what she can do in them," Kane mumbled.

Serena shot him a warning look. "Whatever you have to do is fine, Ray."

"We'll try to save them if we can. We'll line your feet in plastic bags to keep them dry," Ray continued, smiling at her. All the rescue team seemed to be smiling at her. Not that Kane blamed them. She was beautiful, especially as she removed her boots without saying a word. "We're on horseback, so we'll pack out as much as possible. The rest will have to wait until spring."

"I don't need anything but my purse and the dress

bags," she said, the competent, strong-willed dress designer re-emerging.

"Dress bags?" Ray asked.

"Those bulky white things hanging on the bunk," Kane answered. "And trust me, she won't leave the cabin without them."

* * *

Even though Serena's ribs ached more than they had yesterday, she didn't complain. She didn't want to be the reason they had to slow down. Still, she blew out a breath. Unfortunately, it hung on the chilly air.

"We're almost there, Serena." Jake Porter kept offering her encouragement as they traveled on horseback along the snow-covered trail, mile after mile, hour after hour. "Warm enough?"

"Toasty and dry in these clothes you guys loaned me." She appreciated his humor and upbeat attitude, not to mention his killer smile and blue eyes, but she was ready to get there. Wherever "there" might be. "Thanks."

Kane rode thirty yards behind her with one of the wedding dress bags. The others were spread among the rescuers. She smiled at him.

He smiled back and gave her the thumbs-up sign. He was happy. Why wouldn't he be?

They were on their way back to civilization with forced-air heating and indoor plumbing. She was safe.

So why did it feel as if she were riding to her doom?

Serena concentrated on the path in front of her. The rows of trees stood like sentries on the sides of the trail. As they came to a swinging bridge over the Lochsa River, the hair on the back of her neck stood up, and she gripped the reins tightly. She released her breath when the horse knew what to do and crossed without incident. They continued up the trail another two hundred yards until they reached...a trailhead.

Her breath caught in her throat.

"Welcome to Eagle Mountain Trailhead." Ray, who led the group, glanced back and grinned.

"We're here?" she asked.

"I told you we were close," Jake said.

She patted the horse with her gloved hand. "I thought you were trying to keep me motivated."

He grinned. "That, too."

"You guys did a good job." A bittersweet relief washed over her. Now, she could go home. She'd also have to say goodbye to Kane. Her chest tightened at the thought. "Thank you."

Serena emerged from the path and saw trucks, SUVs, police cars, and four media vans with satellite dishes crammed into the gravel pullout. A uniformed official helped her off the horse.

Belle and Charlie stood behind a taped-off section and waved to her. Serena waved back, her heart so happy to see familiar faces. She couldn't wait for one of Belle's trademark hugs.

"Your boyfriend will be here in a minute," Ray said, standing beside her.

"My boyfriend? No, he's my"—*what was he?*—"pilot."

Ray looked from Serena to Kane, who was glowering as he rode from the trail, and gave a masculine-sounding grunt. "Right."

A few reporters barked questions at her. Cameras flashed. She crossed her arms over her chest as if to shield herself.

"Ignore them," Ray advised, placing a protective arm around her back. "You can decide later if you want to talk to the media."

She inhaled deeply, the cold, icy air stinging her lungs as it had been doing during the entire ride, only it felt sharper this time for some reason. "Why are they here?"

"The two of you made headlines," he explained.

Kane stood next to them. She fought the urge to scoot closer to him.

"Slow news day, huh?" he asked.

"You know it." Ray laughed. "Come on. Let's get you guys inside the trailer."

Serena hesitated. Life hadn't stopped with their disappearance. Only their lives. Now, everything would probably change back once she stepped inside the trailer.

Was that what she wanted?

No. The answer resonated through her.

She glanced at Kane, wanting to see a sign that things would stay the same as they had been at the cabin. The chances were slim, but still, she had hoped.

"Ready, Serena?" he said.

Serena, not Blondie.

Too late. She felt like a concrete block had taken the place of her heart. Things had already changed.

* * *

Four microphones, each with a different channel—eight, thirteen, seventeen, and twenty-three—and four digital voice recorders rested on the table in front of Kane. Serena sat next to him. Four cameras pointed in their direction.

Talk about overkill. One would have been too many.

Kane leaned back in his chair at the community medical center in Missoula, where they'd been taken for checkups after being debriefed and returning their borrowed winter gear. All he wanted was for this press conference about their non-newsworthy experience to end.

"Well, I couldn't exactly wear one of the wedding dresses," Serena said, answering yet another stupid question.

The audience, consisting of a handful of journalists, four television reporters, and two high school students, laughed. But the entire White House

Press Corps could have been present and the result would have been the same. In her borrowed surgical scrubs and hair that hadn't been washed in days, she captivated the media. Kane, too. He forced himself not to stare. It wasn't easy. She shone, tossing out witty sound bites like Halloween candy.

Admiration welled in him. She'd been through so much, yet she'd demonstrated such grace and grit in dealing with everything today. Everything since Sunday. Saying goodbye wouldn't be fun even though it had to be done.

"Though Kane suggested I should," Serena added.

Her confidence bloomed under the spotlight. He'd seen the same thing at the bridal show.

Super Serena.

But Kane missed the woman he'd gotten to know at the cabin. He hadn't seen a glimpse of her since they'd stepped into the trailer earlier. Actually, not since they'd left the cabin with the rescue team.

Where had she gone?

"Were you scared when you had to land on a snow-covered meadow, Kane?" a reporter in the second row asked.

A yes or no answer wouldn't satisfy the perched vultures. They would keep asking questions until they got a print-worthy quote. Kane didn't want to waste time. He decided to take a page out of Serena's playbook and give the reporters what they wanted.

"There can be an element of fear whenever

something goes wrong in the cockpit. But you're so busy reacting that emotions take a back seat. At least until you realize the plane is barreling toward a dense forest of trees and there's nothing you can do to stop it. Then, yeah, you're scared."

"Were you scared, Serena?" the same reporter asked.

"I was terrified. I kept praying Kane was as good a pilot as he said." She glanced sideways at him and smiled. "Turns out he is."

Her compliment made Kane feel so good. He sat straighter as if showing people she was right, before realizing what he'd done and leaning back again.

"How would you describe your relationship with each other after your ordeal together?" a woman in the back yelled.

He thought about sleeping with his chest pressed against her back. Or the next day when he'd kissed her for the first time and she'd surprised him by kissing him back. Then when she'd sat on his lap last night and asked him to kiss her. His temperature jumped ten degrees.

"Want to take this one?" Serena asked, apprehension clear in her eyes.

He remembered her pseudo-boyfriend, her insecurity, and her need to project a positive image. She might have been Super Serena, but she wanted help with the question. He wasn't about to turn her down. Kane nodded.

"First, I'd like to clarify something," he said. "Ordeal doesn't exactly describe what we went through. There were no hysterics. We had little choice where we landed, but we kept our cool. We had what we needed to be comfortable—a warm place to stay, water to drink, and food to eat. Serena might look like a city girl, but she knew how to survive in the wilderness. She kept trying to get a signal on her cell phone, and that led to our rescue. The swift action of the search and rescue team got us out of the wilderness in hours. Wouldn't you agree, Serena?"

"It was kind of fun. Well, except the night a pack of wolves paid us a visit."

"You're lucky they only dropped by one night." The on-site incident commander, Logan Michaels, sat to Kane's left and drank coffee as if his life depended on the caffeine to stay awake. No doubt he hadn't slept in a while. "Those wolves and their incessant howling drove out a team of field researchers a couple of years ago."

"Then it's good that we were found before the wolves returned." As Kane spoke, reporters scribbled notes. "As for your question, Serena James started out as a passenger, a wedding dress designer from Boston. But she's so much more than what she does for a living. Serena never gave up or gave in, even when she was a little worried. She deserves full credit for making our location known to authorities so we could be found. I'm proud to call her my"—*girlfriend* came to mind, which surprised him. The term sounded way too natural and stable for someone who didn't want any commitments—"friend."

"Thanks, Kane." Her gaze, full of gratitude and warmth, met his. "I consider you my friend, too."

He didn't want to be her friend. He wanted to be so much more, but that wasn't possible.

"What do you plan on doing now?" another reporter asked.

Serena turned her attention back to the crowd. "I'm flying home to Boston and getting right back to work designing wedding gowns."

"What about you, Kane?" the same reporter asked.

He thought about everything he'd lost in Gold Meadows—his home, his livelihood, his heart. No, he'd almost lost that, but not quite. The other things, however...

"I need to talk to the insurance company and the forest service about my plane and to someone in Seattle about the contaminated fuel. That'll probably occupy my time for a while."

And that was a good thing.

He needed the distraction so he could put Serena James out of his mind. Because that was exactly where she belonged, even if his heart didn't agree.

GROUP CHAT #6

Serena: *Hey! Thanks for all the concern. I'm safe. Love you three so much. xoxo*

Jane: *Oh, thank goodness. I watched the press conference. Even in those scrubs, you looked amazing.*

Elle: *Yes, and I was so impressed by the way you answered the questions.*

Kelsey: *You were a total pro up there.*

Serena: *Thanks. If dress designing doesn't work out, maybe I can get a role on a medical drama.*

Kelsey: *The dress designing is already working out, and the way you went above and beyond for those wedding dresses you brought with you will have clients clamoring to have you design their gowns.*

Serena: *I wish, but this is just my fifteen minutes of fame.*

Elle: *I doubt that.*

Jane: *People were talking about it at the coffee shop.*

Kelsey: *I'm just relieved you're okay. You are okay, right? That wasn't just PR?*

Serena: *I have some bruised ribs and bruises from the seat belt, but I'm healing. The doctor isn't concerned at all.*

Jane: *So glad to hear that.*

Elle: *That pilot of yours is attractive.*

Jane: *I thought you hated men.*

Elle: *I can still see, and Kane is a nice piece of eye candy.*

Kelsey: *He is. Even Will mentioned something about being jealous if Kane was my pilot.*

Serena: *Well, I'm sure Rupert isn't jealous at all. I read the entire chat and know Belle told Kelsey about him breaking up with me. I'm sorry for not saying anything when it happened. I have no excuse other than ones that made sense in my head at the time. I'd rather not go into those reasons now, but I promise I will. I'm sorry.*

Elle: *No need to apologize. Trust me, I know how badly breakups hurt, especially when you think you'll spend the rest of your life with someone. When you're ready, we're here.*

Jane: *What Elle said. We're always here for you. But right now, you need to rest and get home.*

Kelsey: *That's right. And let us know your flight info so I can arrange a ride home for you. It's the least we can do after everything you've been through.*

Serena: *Thank you so much!*

Serena wiped the tears from her eyes. Telling them had been easier than she'd thought, but these women were closer to her than her own family. Of course they would understand. She typed her flight numbers and times and then pressed send.

Now, all she had to do was see how the wedding dresses she'd brought with her had fared. Serena crossed her fingers.

CHAPTER ELEVEN

All Serena wanted to do was shower and then plop onto one of the full-size beds in Belle's motel room. Instead, she stared at the closet, her pulse picking up.

"We can do this tomorrow, darlin'." Belle's eyes clouded with concern. "You look tired."

Tired didn't begin to describe how Serena felt. She wasn't sure whether the ride out, the press conference, or pretending she and Kane were just friends had been more taxing, but she couldn't crawl between the motel bedsheets yet. "I need to take care of this."

With purposeful steps, she went to the closet and opened the door where six no-longer-white dress bags hung. The small space smelled like the cabin. Serena fought the rush of memories of her and Kane. She'd only said goodbye to him an hour ago, but after his constant companionship, it seemed like days. "The smoke from the woodstove seeped into the bags. I hope it's the bags, not the dresses. Otherwise…"

"Don't borrow worry." Belle held on to six new pink dress bags a local bridal store had sold her to transport the dresses back to Boston tomorrow. "Trust me on this one."

"I will." Serena fought the tears stinging her eyes. She'd been struggling with an internal battle and felt guilty. So many people were worried about her. So many people had endured the cold, snowy weather to look for them. But Serena wished she were still at the cabin with Kane, where she could be herself. "Having you here means so much. I don't know what I would have done if I'd walked into that trailer and only seen strangers."

"You had Kane with you."

Not really. "It's not the same as having someone you love there. Thank you for coming all this way to be with me."

Belle laid the pink bags on the bed and enveloped Serena in one of her trademark hugs. "I'm glad to be here, darlin'."

Belle's perfume comforted Serena like the smell of her favorite chocolate cake. Her friends were what really mattered. What had happened at the cabin was simply…a dream.

Yet she'd felt more real, more alive, more herself there. Kane's praise of her courage and uncomplaining attitude had been real, too. Not like a dream at all.

"I kept your parents and your sorority sisters updated."

"Thanks. I appreciate that." And then Serena remembered what she'd read in the group chat. The air evaporated from Serena's lungs, and she struggled to breathe. "I heard you called Rupert."

"Let's not worry about that now," Belle said. "We'll have plenty of time to talk about things later. Once you're rested and back home. Okay?"

Serena swallowed around the snowball-size lump in her throat as she felt herself drifting back to how she'd been before the time in the cabin. Kane never would have let her put off explaining everything the way her friends and Belle had. "Thank you again."

"Anytime, darlin'."

Serena unzipped the first bag with a hesitant hand. All the dress bags looked alike. She had no idea which gown was inside which bag. Each catch of the zipper felt like a countdown to the moment of truth. Afraid to look, she closed her eyes and pushed the bag off and away.

Belle released a rebel yell.

Serena's eyelids sprang open. She stared at a perfectly white wedding dress made of chiffon with crystals sprayed across the gown. "Thank goodness."

"It looks perfect."

She studied the gown as if inspecting a perfect jewel for a flaw. She left no thread unexamined but found no problems. Oh, the dress was a little crushed and a lot wrinkled, but nothing a bit of steaming or careful pressing wouldn't fix.

"It's perfect." Serena sniffed the fabric. "And no smoke smell, either. I don't believe it."

Belle grinned. "Believe it."

Serena put the gown into a new bag and zipped it up.

"On to the next one."

She unzipped the bag. Not even halfway down, she stopped.

Belle grimaced. "That's not just smoke I smell."

"Mildew maybe."

"Let's see how bad it is." Belle gasped when the dress came out of the bag. "It's…"

"Ruined." Tears prickled Serena's eyes when she saw the water and dirt spots on the diamond-white satin with a champagne tulle lace overlay. Small holes had destroyed the Alencon lace around the neckline. Had a mouse gotten inside somehow? "At least it's a sample dress from the new collection, not a custom gown."

Like Calista's dress.

Don't borrow worry.

Easier said than done.

With a heavy heart, she continued. To her surprise, the next two dresses came out fine. One was a sleeveless silk with a cutaway skirt, and the other was satin with embellished lace on the bodice and sleeves. Both were wrinkled but still fresh-smelling. Neither, however, was Calista's dress.

When Serena came to the next dress bag, her heart

pounded in her ears. She was almost afraid to go on. Unzipping the next bag, she recognized the beading on the bodice.

Her hand froze. "This is Calista's dress."

Belle sucked in a breath.

The zipper went down three more inches, and Serena's heart plummeted. The air whooshed from her lungs. She sagged against the doorframe.

"What is it?" Belle asked.

"Calista's dress." Serena's voice cracked. "It's ruined."

As she pulled the dress bag away, a mouse fell out. Belle screeched and jumped back. Serena was too dejected to care.

She stared at what had once been her most exquisite creation. The strapless A-line corset-back gown with delustered satin alternating with rows of scalloped lace had a fairy-tale feel yet a strong, contemporary silhouette. Swarovski crystals, bugle beads, and seed beads embellished the bodice. The dress had been designed with Calista in mind, but now...

Forget calling what remained a wedding gown. The wet, dirty, smelly, and holey dress looked like a farce— a bad joke gone too far. It wasn't fair.

Serena fought back the tears. She had to be strong and hold herself together. She needed to show Belle she could handle this. But inside, she trembled, a potent combination of failure and disappointment grabbing hold of her. No doubt there was probably, finally, shock from the entire event.

She longed to have Kane here, for him to tell her that everything would be okay and help her fix this the way he had everything else since crash-landing in the meadow.

"You'll have to use one of the gowns you have back at the studio for her," Belle said calmly.

"No." Serena raised her chin. "I promised Calista I would take care of her dress. I owe her a one-of-a-kind creation, and that's what she'll have."

"Calista's wedding is less than two weeks away," Belle said. "You've already lost this week and still have other obligations to meet, darlin'."

"Don't worry about a thing. I can do this."

And Serena would—once she'd showered and slept.

* * *

As fingers of the sunrise broke over the mountains to the east, Serena sat in a corner booth at the coffee shop next door to the hotel in Missoula, Montana. She warmed her cold hands on a steaming cup of coffee.

"Mind if I join you?"

The familiar male voice brought a sensation of pleasure rippling through her. Kane. She'd missed him so much already, which made no sense. She'd only spent a night away from him, but what a night.

Sleep hadn't come easy at all. She'd tried to take advantage of the insomnia to think about Calista's dress. That had only made Serena anxious and lonely.

She fought the urge to throw herself against his chest and cry about the ruined wedding dress for her friend's upcoming fairy-tale wedding. In her mind, he would hold her and make her feel better like no one else could. And then she remembered. Kane wasn't into dresses and didn't believe in fairy tales.

She raised her coffee and took a sip. "Sure."

Kane placed his coffee cup on the table and sat across from her. He wore jeans, a green shirt, and a brown leather jacket that made his eyes look hazel. His hair was damp as if straight from the shower. His razor stubble was gone, replaced by smooth skin she longed to feel rubbing against her cheek.

"Sleep well?" he asked.

"Not as well as I thought I would."

"Me neither."

Clean and casual, he looked entirely too delectable. She wanted a taste. Instead, she dug into another bite of her buttermilk pancakes with maple syrup.

Kane whistled. "That's some breakfast."

She eyed her plate of scrambled eggs, pancakes, bacon, and fruit. "I was hungry."

"A couple of days of granola bars, honey-roasted peanuts, pretzels, and crackers will make you crave a real breakfast."

"I wasn't tired of our food at the cabin." She

remembered the many wrappers that had piled up during their meals. "I liked the cabin. Well, except for the wolves, the mice, and the outhouse. There's something to be said for flushing toilets."

His smile reached his eyes, and her heart beat faster. "You didn't go away."

"Excuse me?"

"The Serena I got to know at the cabin. I thought she'd disappeared, especially after Super Serena wowed the media with her sparkling brilliance."

"Brilliance?"

"I needed sunglasses, Blondie."

She smiled at his use of the nickname. "I was trying to get through the press conference the best way I knew."

The only way she knew how was to revert to what she did best: putting up a perfect façade. Maybe Super Serena did exist.

"You did great," he said. "You're back in your element."

"I don't feel like it," she admitted. "I feel like the only scarlet-and-gold cap sleeve on a rack of strapless diamond whites."

Kane raised his cup and took a sip. "That bad, huh?"

"You have no idea what I just said."

"Nope, but I can tell from your tone that you feel out of place, and that matters to me."

"Why does it matter?"

"I like you."

"You like me?" Not good enough. "Like me how?"

A beat passed. "As I said at the press conference, you're my friend, Serena."

Her heart deflated a little even though being just friends made sense. She no longer wanted to settle for Mr. Right Now. "You're mine, too, but…"

The word hung out there. She was afraid to say more. Still, she might not get another chance, so she pushed back her shoulders.

"What happened at the cabin…"

"It was…"

"Nice?" she offered.

"Great."

"Yes, great. I didn't know how you felt."

"I like you, Blondie. I'm attracted to you, but we want different things."

"We do." And taking what happened at the cabin any further made no sense. Kane understood that, and so did Serena. But the thought of never seeing him again hurt.

"I just came in for a quick cup of coffee." He pushed back his chair. "So maybe I'll see you around."

A brush-off.

"Planning a trip to Boston?" she asked lightly.

Stupid question. He didn't plan.

His gaze met hers. "I could be."

Oh, heavens.

Friends, she reminded herself. They wanted

different things. "Then I'll see you in Boston sometime."

He nodded once.

Her heart thudded. She couldn't wait.

"I've got an appointment with the forest service this morning about my plane." He stood. "Have a safe flight home."

She hated to see him go. "Good luck with your plane and, well, everything else."

He leaned over and kissed her on the forehead. Nothing more than a friendly brush of his lips. "Goodbye, Blondie."

"Bye, Kane."

He left the coffee shop and got into a nondescript blue sedan. As he backed out, he waved at her. She waved back.

Mr. Right, Mr. Right Now, or Mr. Wrong? Serena didn't care. A sigh escaped from her lips. She hoped "sometime" came soon because she really wanted to see him again.

* * *

"Thank you." As Belle took her suitcase from Charlie at Logan International Airport in Boston, her hand brushed his. Tingles shot up her arm. She ignored them the same way she paid no attention to the warmth settling in the center of her chest. "I don't know how I would have made it through without you...your friendship."

"I feel the same way." His gaze held hers, and her heart melted a little. "I'll give you and Serena a ride home. That way, we can be more careful with the dress bags."

His continued generosity touched Belle. She glanced at the restroom to see if Serena was out yet. "That's sweet of you, but a friend of Serena's arranged for a limo to take us home."

Charlie's smile didn't reach his eyes. "Riding home in style."

"Serena deserves it."

"She does." He raised Belle's hand to his lips and kissed it. "But so do you."

The heat in her cheeks matched the temperature of the blood racing through her veins. Blushing at her age? But she wasn't used to a man switching attention from a younger woman to her. Belle pulled her hand away from his and adjusted the purse strap on her shoulder.

"When can I see you again?" he asked.

She hesitated. Sure, Charlie was an attractive and wealthy man. She enjoyed his company. They'd relied on each other during the stress-filled days when Serena and Kane were missing and became closer. But now that the crisis was over, seeing him again might not be such a good idea. He was nice, but Belle didn't want to lead him on.

"That hard to answer, huh?" he added, humor lacing his words.

Maybe she shouldn't put too much thought into the decision. Belle smiled. "Give me a call, darlin'."

That was the best she could come up with right now.

Anticipation filled his brown eyes. "I will."

His lighthearted grin took ten years off his face. Her heart sank. She was already nine years older than Charlie. Add ten to nine and...

She didn't want to think about the total, especially when that was all in her head. Nine years wasn't that much, was it?

He wrapped his arms around her and squeezed. His hug shouldn't have surprised her; they'd held and comforted each other in Idaho. Support was no longer necessary, yet a part of Belle didn't want it to end.

Uh-oh. She was acting like someone who'd just met a new beau. Maybe this wasn't such a good idea.

She stepped out of Charlie's embrace. "I need to get Serena home. She looks as if she hasn't slept a wink, and she's been so quiet. Do you know if anything happened between her and Kane that we don't know about?"

"Kane said they were friends."

"Friends like us?" Belle asked, wondering if Serena was keeping more secrets.

"He didn't elaborate, but you know I want to be more than your friend, Belle."

She nodded. The way Kane looked at Serena

reminded Belle of the way Charlie looked at her. The elder Wiley was a true gentleman, but the younger seemed to be more of a ladies' man. That could spell only one thing for Belle's already heartbroken young designer.

TROUBLE.

CHAPTER TWELVE

Serena returned to Boston on a thankfully uneventful commercial flight. Even the pink dress bags arrived in perfect condition. She struggled to find a sense of normalcy. Something she still grappled with on Monday as she sat in her studio, trying to reconstruct Calista's dress.

Nothing was working. Serena didn't have enough of the diamond-white delustered satin left, so she used a regular white satin instead. This fabric, however, had bluer overtones and didn't drape as well as the original. The seed and bugle beads disappeared against the satin's higher sheen.

Should she use more crystals or a tinted lace? Both would change the look of the dress.

Who was she kidding? The fabric already did. Maybe she should come up with a new design.

Tossing a piece of embellished tulle onto her worktable, Serena glanced at the giant calendar hanging on the wall. Twelve days until Calista's wedding. Two fittings would need to be scheduled. Time for alterations in between. Serena had the Brodeur bridesmaids flying into town this weekend for measurements. She couldn't forget about the dress fitting on Tuesday and the other fitting planned for next Thursday. And then there was Calista's surprise shower on Wednesday night.

Ugh. How will I fit it all in?

Serena rubbed her pounding head.

Closing her eyes, she tried to imagine Calista's finished wedding gown but saw the cabin instead. Serena could smell smoke and pine and hear the rattle of the wind against the windows. If only she could be there with Kane instead of here alone. Maybe she could channel the cabin to make a fairy-tale dress.

Not good. Serena opened her eyes and glanced around her studio. How come what she'd always wanted no longer seemed enough?

A knock sounded on the door that separated the studio from the rest of the shop. She checked her watch. Her next appointment was over an hour away. "Come in."

"You need to go to the lobby. I have a new cake for you to taste." Pink-and-purple chopsticks, most likely painted by Nadia's twin daughters, secured the pile of blond hair on the top of her head. In her well-worn jeans and blue sweater that matched the color of her eyes, she looked more like a college student than a mom and talented cake artist. "It's chocolate."

"My favorite."

"I know." Nadia never brought slices of cake into the studio due to all the white fabric. The petite baker hopped up and sat on a nearby stool. "How's it going?"

Serena ignored the calendar and forced a smile. "Good."

"You've been working so hard since you got back."

"Lots of winter weddings. And Calista's gown." Serena picked up one of the bodice panels. "I wish..."

"What do you wish?"

"Nothing really. Do-overs aren't possible."

"A lot of us wish they were." Nadia sighed. "What would you change if you could?"

"Nothing."

"Come on," Nadia challenged. "You're the one who brought it up. There must be something."

If Serena could be herself with Kane, maybe she should try to be more honest with her closest friends.

"I would have told you all about Rupert as soon as it happened." She glanced at her worktable. "I should have told you all."

"You did finally tell us the truth," Nadia said. "That couldn't have been easy for you."

"Or any of you." Serena looked up at her. "I really am sorry. I didn't want to disappoint any of you."

Nadia smiled softly. "Just remember, next time, we're here for you. We love you."

"I will."

"You'd better." Nadia sounded every bit a mom. "Now, go get a slice of cake."

"I'd love to." Serena knew the baker, a diabetic, couldn't taste all her own creations and relied on others for their opinions. "And thanks."

"For what?"

"For being my friend."

"Anytime." Nadia beamed. "I'm going to see who else wants a slice."

Serena made her way into the reception area. The front desk was empty. She picked up a slice of chocolate cake with a raspberry fruit filling.

As she raised her fork, the scents of chocolate and icing filled her nostrils. Okay, things could have been a lot worse right now. She took a bite. The chocolate flavor exploded in her mouth. The not-too-sweet raspberry filling complemented the cake and icing perfectly.

As she ate, the doorbell rang. With a mouthful of cake, she opened the door.

Kane stood on the porch in a pair of black pants, a black turtleneck, and his brown leather jacket.

She choked on the bite in her mouth.

His dark eyes narrowed. "You okay, Blondie?"

She nodded, struggling to swallow. "Cake."

"Can I have a taste?"

Serena scooped a bite with her fork and fed it to him.

"That's the best cake I've ever tasted." He smiled at her.

Her heart thudded. And that was when she knew.

She wasn't just Kane's friend. She was in love with him. Even though she'd only known him for a few days, they'd been the most intense days of her life. He was wrong for her and didn't fit any of her plans or her life, but she didn't care. All she wanted was to be with him.

That realization scared her to death.

"You look good," he said.

"Thanks." The appreciation in his eyes made her forget she'd been up half the night, hadn't showered this morning, and wasn't wearing lip gloss. "Want to come in?"

"That's why I'm here."

Her cheeks heated. She stepped aside, and he entered the lobby, looking around.

"Very wedding-like."

She laughed. He had that same what-have-I-gotten-myself-into expression as he'd worn in Seattle. But she was grateful he was here. "How did things go with your plane?"

"I can't get it out of Gold Meadows until spring, but the insurance company declared it a total loss based on the pictures and the report."

"Kane." She reached for him but pulled back her arm. "I'm so sorry."

"No worries. I'll buy another."

"And fly away again." The words flew out before she could stop them.

He nodded.

"When do you plan to do that?" she asked lightly, trying to sound like it didn't matter to her while wondering if he could hear her voice over the pounding of her heart.

"As soon as I can."

Her clothing seemed to have been stitched too tightly, and she couldn't breathe. Not that she should have been surprised by his answer. He'd never pretended to be anything but what he was.

He handed her a white medium-size shopping bag. "For you."

She set the plate of cake on a table, peeked inside, and saw white tissue paper.

"Go on," he urged.

Serena pushed aside the paper and saw something gray and white. She pulled the stuffed animal out and smiled. "A wolf."

"A little something to remember your adventure in Gold Meadows."

She would never forget it. Or him. She cuddled the wolf. "That was so thoughtful of you. Thank you, Kane."

He hooked his thumb through a belt loop. "Do you have time for a cup of coffee?"

Yes. She wanted to see him, even if things weren't perfect.

No. He would just leave again, so why bother?

"I, um, have an appointment in an hour, and I should be working."

"My dad told me what happened to a few of your dresses."

"You've been talking to your dad?"

"I'm staying with him."

"Good." Maybe they could start working out some of their differences. Both men needed each other. She smiled. "He must be happy to have you around."

Kane shrugged. "If you've been working that much, you probably need caffeine or something besides cake to eat."

"There's nothing wrong with cake."

"Nope, but you can't live on cake alone. You need coffee, too." He grinned. "Come on. I promise I won't keep you long."

The problem was she wanted him to keep her forever. She swallowed hard.

"What do you say, Blondie?" he asked.

Serena wanted to say yes.

Maybe she could convince him that they would be good for each other. That he could find what he needed right here in Boston. Or maybe not. And he would fly off, chasing his notion of freedom again.

She stared at the wolf in her arms. "One cup. Then I have to get back to work."

* * *

Walking along the sidewalk with Serena felt weird to Kane. The traffic on the street, the squeal of brakes, and the blare of horns were a far cry from the snow-swallowed silence of the wilderness. The smells of exhaust and garbage made him miss the fresh pine and smoke scents. But he was happy to be with Serena. He'd missed her so much that when he had seen the wolf in a store window in Missoula, he'd bought it for her without a moment's hesitation.

"We weren't gone that long," he said. "But I'm not used to being back in the real world yet."

"Me neither." Serena looked up at him, big round sunglasses covering her eyes. She wore a trendy wool coat, black boots, and a knee-length skirt. A multicolored cap covered her blond hair. "I never really paid attention to the different noises in the city before, but now I miss the quiet of the woods. I keep thinking about the cabin."

And he'd been thinking about her. Too much.

What she had said kept swirling in his mind.

"Like me how?"

Serena's words and the look in her eyes at the restaurant that morning had haunted Kane for the past four days. He had thought being away from her would keep her out of his thoughts and off his mind.

Wrong.

Which was why he needed to see her. To prove to himself that these strong feelings for her meant nothing, that he was hooked on a silly fantasy and nothing more.

"So…" she said.

He stopped on the curb, waiting for the light to change. "You've been busy."

"Yes. The work keeps piling up." She shoved her gloved hands into her pockets, reminding Kane of when she had worn his gloves, and smiled. "It's been hard getting back into designing, but I'm checking things off the to-do list."

Kane had wondered how she had been managing since returning home. He'd pictured her in full press-conference mode. Super Serena to the max. But he could see now that he'd been wrong about that. Despite the usual perfection of her appearance and even the smile on her face, she appeared tired, stressed, and a little sad. Instead of those things making her less beautiful, they only made him care for her more.

Real, not fantasy.

Self-preservation told him to run away as fast as he could. He could find a new plane anywhere. But Kane knew how vulnerable Serena James was. He didn't want to hurt her, and though she probably wouldn't admit it, he got the feeling she needed him.

They entered a corner coffeehouse where they ordered drinks to go. Serena picked up a sandwich, too.

"What's really wrong, Blondie?" he asked on the walk back to the shop. "You've got a smile on your face, but you don't look happy."

"What do you mean? I've got almost everything a girl could want. Of course I'm happy."

"I'm not buying it." He removed her glasses. "I see

a woman who's tired and stressed."

"I worked late last night and forgot to eat dinner and breakfast." She flashed him a brilliant smile. "I'm hungry, but okay."

"Good thing you bought a sandwich." He tucked her sunglasses into his jacket pocket so he could see her entire face. "But a person doesn't have to feel good to smile if they know how to flex their facial muscles. That's what my mom used to say when she was trying to get me to admit I'd had a bad day."

Serena sipped her latte. "Did it work?"

"Usually." Kane wished his mom were here so he could talk to her about Serena. "Why don't you just tell me what's going on? Unless you want me to start guessing."

"Please don't." She sounded horrified at the thought.

Chalk another one up to Mom. A smile pulled at his lips. "So…"

"The biggest issue right now is Calista's dress," Serena explained. "She's my friend and the florist who has a shop at Belle's brownstone. Her dress was one that got ruined. Destroyed, actually. Her wedding is a week from Saturday, and I'm not even close to having something ready so I can fit her for alterations."

"You need help."

"I can do it myself."

"Can you?" he asked. "Or is that Super Serena talking?"

"There is no Super Serena. Just me. And I can do

it." She sounded capable and sure of herself.

He wasn't buying it. "You can do it if you don't sleep or eat or waste a single moment."

Her mouth formed a perfect O. "We hardly know each other, yet you seem to know me the best of all. How is that possible?"

"It's a gift." He studied her, trying to see beneath that perfect façade. "Let me help you."

She drew back. "You?"

The offer had been an impulse, but Kane enjoyed hearing the laughter in her voice and knowing he'd been the reason for it. If worse came to worst, he'd get to spend some time with her. No regrets there. "Yeah, me."

"What do you know about wedding dresses?"

"Less than you know about planes. But I can be an extra pair of hands, a sounding board, someone to bring you food, whatever you need."

"Mr. Right Now?"

Oh man. Kane rocked back onto his heels. "If that's what you want."

She stared at her coffee, and he felt like a jerk. She wanted so much more than he could give her.

"In any case…" She pressed her lips together and met his eyes. "You're leaving."

"I'm not leaving until I find a plane. The right plane. I have a few to look at, but what's a few extra days in Boston if I get to help you?"

Those baby blues of hers widened. "A few days?"

The hope in her voice and the anticipation in her

eyes slammed into him. Suddenly, following through on his offer didn't seem like such a good idea, yet Kane nodded anyway.

"Okay, then," she said with a hesitant grin. "You're hired."

* * *

When Kane had agreed to help Serena, he didn't know what he was getting himself into. He hadn't really cared. What had he promised her? A few days. No big deal.

But helping her out felt good, and they'd kept things platonic, too. He'd offered to help her, not take advantage of her.

"Can you please move that one about three inches to the left?" Serena asked.

But he'd never thought he'd be standing in one of Boston's finest mansions, hanging wedding dresses on the walls of an impressive dining room. "No problem."

And it wasn't.

He enjoyed seeing Super Serena in action. The way she took charge of the decorating for Calista's surprise wedding shower tonight reminded him of a military leader in action. Serena gave him direction with quick, decisive steps. So far, he'd strung wide satin ribbons around the dining room and now was hanging wedding dresses on fancy hangers with big bows.

He moved the dress he was holding the requested three inches. "How's this?"

"Perfect."

Her favorite word.

He had to admit Serena James was pretty perfect herself—just not for him. Despite how much he enjoyed her, they were too different and wanted different things out of life.

Still, Kane had feelings for her, but he wasn't about to hurt her, especially when she was having such a hard time remaking that stupid wedding dress. He would help her, and then he would leave.

"There's one more gown," she said.

"Where do you want it?" he asked.

She pointed to the spot. He moved the stepladder and hung the dress.

Sure, he'd thought about taking things further. But there was no sense in starting something he couldn't finish.

"How's that?" he asked.

"A little to the left."

He'd learned with the seven other dresses not to guesstimate. She'd only make him redo it. "How little?"

"An inch and a half."

Good thing he'd asked. Kane moved the dress, pleased with the work they'd done.

Serena impressed him, as usual. She'd transformed the dining room into the perfect setting for a bridal shower. No wonder people spoke about her creativity with awe. She really was something.

He climbed down from the stepladder. "What do you think?"

She spun around slowly, taking in each dress, all the ribbons, every bow. "It works."

"It's fantastic," he said. "And I'm a guy. I'm not supposed to notice stuff like this. Good job."

She smiled. "You, too."

"You deserve all the credit," he said. "You're the one who came up with the idea and told me what to do."

Something in her eyes changed. "You know, there's been something else I've wanted to tell you to do ever since you came back."

"What?" he asked, intrigued.

"This." She leaned over and kissed him.

The feel of her mouth against his, her lips pressing and probing, made his temperature skyrocket. He'd pretended that this was a fantasy and he hadn't wanted to kiss her. That she hadn't meant much to him.

But he had, and she did.

This was all too real.

She tasted sweet and warm as she moved her lips over his. He wanted more—everything she was willing to give.

Kane brought his arm around her, running his fingers through her hair. He soaked up the feel and taste of her, kissing her as if there were no tomorrow. He felt as if he'd found the place where he belonged and never wanted to leave again. He was finally home.

The kisses continued until she slowly and gently pulled away. Serena stared at him with wide eyes and swollen, thoroughly kissed lips.

"That's what you've been wanting to tell me to do since I came back?" he asked.

She lifted her chin. "Yes."

As he brushed away strands of her bangs that had fallen over her right eye, he smiled. "You're so beautiful, so brave, so perfect."

"You think?"

"I know." He kissed her lightly on the lips. "I might have to stick around Boston a little while longer."

Her smile lit up her face. "There's nothing I'd like more."

GROUP CHAT #7

Serena had typed what felt like a romance novel in the group chat about what had happened with Kane. Well, not every single detail, but enough so she didn't feel like she was keeping another big secret from her three closest friends. She just had one more thing to say.

Serena: *After I kissed him, he said he might stick around Boston longer.*

Jane: *Oh my goodness. This sounds like a movie.*

Elle: *Yes, and Serena is way braver than me.*

Kelsey: *Your time will come, but just be careful, Serena. He's told you what he's like.*

Serena: *I know, but there's something about him.*

Jane: *Irresistible!*

Serena: *Yes. And I just have to see where this goes. It feels right, even if there's no future.*

Jane: *He could change his mind about what he wants.*

Elle: *Or not.*

Kelsey: *He won't find anyone like Serena anyway.*

Elle: *That's true.*

Serena: *You guys!*

Elle: *Just writing the truth. You deserve to be happy.*

Kelsey: *We all do.*

Serena: *I have to get to poker night, which is actually the ruse to get Calista to her surprise wedding shower.*

Kelsey: *Have fun!*

Elle: *We'll want to hear all about it!*

Jane: *Have a slice of cake for me!*

CHAPTER THIRTEEN

With the poker-and-margarita night underway, Serena glanced at the clock on the wall of Rebecca's kitchen. Belle had sent a text saying the guests had arrived for Calista's surprise wedding shower. Now, all they had to do was get the bride-to-be into the dining room.

Good thing part B of Operation Poker Plan was already underway.

Aubrey, a caterer, flipped her long, blond hair behind her shoulder. "I'm all in, too."

Calista gasped as the pile of chips in the center grew taller. "The entire table is all in? That's impossible."

Serena looked at her partners in crime, Aubrey and Rebecca. The others—Nadia and Belle—were busy in the dining room.

"This doesn't make any sense. There aren't that many good hands." Calista's face scrunched. She studied the cards on the table. "Serena never goes all in. Could a certain pilot be leading you to take more risks these days?"

"Maybe."

"You and your hottie flyboy seem pretty chummy," Rebecca said.

"We're getting chummier." Serena took a sip of her margarita, thinking about what had happened earlier. She'd spilled to Kelsey, Jane, and Elle. No reason not to tell her work friends, too. "I kissed him this afternoon."

"And?" Calista asked.

Serena got all tingly inside. "It was absolutely, positively wonderful. My toes curled."

"I'd like to experience a kiss like that," Aubrey said. "That is, if I ever plan to date again."

"You sound like my friend Elle, and I'll tell you what we all tell her. You will," Serena encouraged. "And I hope you find someone who makes your toes curl."

Calista's eyes softened. "It's nice to see you opening up and talking about Kane like this."

"It feels good," Serena admitted. "Hey, don't we need to see who wins this huge pot of chips?"

Rebecca nodded. "Let's see your cards, ladies."

Serena laid her pair of threes on the table. The other two had nothing but a couple of face cards.

"I can't believe you guys went all in on those hands. It's like you wanted to lose." Calista flipped over a full house. "I win."

"Great hand," Aubrey said.

Calista moved the stack of chips in front of her and took a sip from her frozen margarita. "Not a bad haul, but I can't believe how fast the game ended."

Serena nursed her own drink. She still had work to do, and a part of her hoped Kane might stop by. She bit back a sigh. "Luck of the cards."

Calista shuffled the deck. "We have time for another game."

"How does the new buffet look in the dining room, Rebecca?" Aubrey asked.

"I'd like to see it before I head out," Serena added, not wanting to delay part C of the evening's plan. "I do have your wedding dress to finish."

Calista grinned. "I know you've been working hard on it. I have no doubt this new one will be even better and more perfect than the one that got destroyed."

Her friend's confidence told Serena how much Calista believed in her, and she could not let the bride-to-be down. Serena would give her the dress she deserved no matter what it took.

"Let's all go and see it." Rebecca stood.

"But then we're going to play some more." Calista picked up her drink and followed Aubrey.

Rebecca led the way, surreptitiously picking up her camera from the kitchen counter on her way toward the dining room. She crossed the threshold first. Next came Aubrey. Then Calista.

"Surprise!" a group of twenty women yelled.

Flashes from Rebecca's camera blinded Serena, but she kept a smile on her face. The photos would go into a wedding shower album the photographer planned to put together for their friend.

"How did you guys do all this?" Calista asked Serena.

"While we played poker, Belle and Nadia set up and snuck guests into the dining room."

Calista stared, wide-eyed. "I can't believe how quiet everyone was."

Nadia smiled. "Belle threatened some nasty Southern torture to anyone who so much as sneezed."

"We Southerners know how to control a crowd, darlin'," Belle purred.

"I had no idea," Calista admitted. "Though everyone going all in at once was a little strange. But it's all so wonderful. Look at those wedding dresses hanging on the walls. Amazing."

Rebecca handed Calista a fresh margarita. "Using the dresses as decorations was Serena's brilliant idea."

Serena appreciated the compliment. "Well, I couldn't exactly ask our florist for help, now could I? I had to come up with something on my own."

The same way she would with Calista's dress.

"The gown I wore when I married Matthew is next to the window," Belle said.

Calista turned and sighed. "Lovely."

"Dated, but still pretty and so tiny," Belle said with a grin. "There wasn't quite so much of me back then."

"We wouldn't want you any other way than you are now," Aubrey said, and the rest of them agreed.

Belle sniffled. "What would I do without you girls?"

"I don't know what I'd do without any of you. Thank you." Calista blinked. "This is so much more than I ever imagined having."

Everyone knew that Calista hadn't had the easiest of times, but things in her life had changed for the better since she'd rented a shop with Belle and fallen in love with Jason Townley.

As Serena thought about Calista's past, her thoughts strayed right back to Kane. He didn't seem to be in any hurry to leave Boston because he wanted to help her. He'd kissed her back. That had to mean he had feelings for her, but she had to be patient. She couldn't force Kane to love her, and she didn't want to force him to run, either. She just wanted him to tell her how he felt. She imagined her and Kane as a couple like Calista and Jason. The image filled Serena with warmth.

"A toast." Serena raised her glass. "To Calista and Jason. May their love for one another never stop growing. Even after the wedding, the honeymoon, and the kids."

Everyone laughed.

"Kids?" Calista teased. "I may need another drink."

"Best wishes on your journey toward your happily ever after," Serena added.

"Hear, hear!" The guests raised their margarita glasses. "To Calista and Jason."

"Thank you," Calista mouthed.

Nodding, Serena smiled, though celebrating was the last thing she should have been doing right now. Calista trusted her to finish the dress, but Serena wouldn't have missed tonight for the world. Even if being here meant working another late night.

Her friend was worth it.

Calista deserved the perfect wedding gown for her perfect wedding. Serena wouldn't let her down.

* * *

Saturday, Serena took her work home with her, hoping the change of scenery would spark her creativity. So far, it hadn't. By that night, she was overwhelmed and exhausted. She glanced at the clock. Nine o'clock. All she wanted to do was to go to sleep, but she couldn't. Not when she needed to work on Calista's wedding dress. If Serena finished the gown tonight, she could do the embellishments tomorrow and be ready for a fitting on Monday. That would allow plenty of time for alterations.

Kane stood behind her and massaged her tense shoulders. "You're all bunched up, Blondie."

She almost moaned with relief. His fingers felt so good against all the knots that had built up from working so hard. "It's been a long week, but your being here to help has made it better."

"I'm happy to help." He kissed her neck. "I was thinking I could spend the night here."

Her insides fluttered and then tensed. "Tonight?"

"I could take better care of you if I was on-site, so to speak."

"No." The word flew from her mouth. "I'm too busy, too distracted. I want your first night here to be perfect."

His mouth tightened. "Why does everything always have to be perfect with you?"

Because that's how things should be when I tell you I love you. She couldn't tell him that. "It just does."

Great, she sounded like a spoiled little kid.

"I'm not trying to push you into something you're not ready for, Blondie." His gaze held hers. "I only want to take care of you the best way I know how."

She looked at the mannequin wearing Calista's almost finished dress. "Not tonight."

"Why not?"

"I don't have time."

"I'm not asking for your time. Just a space on your couch tonight."

She shook her head. "I... That's not good enough."

He stepped away from her. "You mean I'm not good enough."

"I never said that."

"You didn't have to." The hurt in his voice clawed at her heart. "You're too busy chasing your vision of perfection to see something right and real in front of you. Can't you cut me some slack?"

"Slack?" Her voice sharpened. Serena had thought Kane understood her, but he didn't. He couldn't. "I have to finish the dress."

"Or kill yourself trying." He picked up a piece of lace and waved it in the air. Though the lace was white, she didn't think he was surrendering. "Is a dress worth all this? The sun will still rise tomorrow if you don't get it done."

"I have to have it done."

"Then ask for some help." He dropped the fabric. Tenderness filled his eyes. "Your friends would be here in a heartbeat."

"Calista trusts me. She's counting on *me*," Serena explained, feeling as if everything she held dear was about to unravel. "I have it under control."

"I'm sorry, Blondie, but you don't."

She stiffened.

"You have to stop pretending. Look at the toll this is taking on you. Your health. Your life. It's destroying you. I won't let you keep this up."

"You won't let me?" Her temper flared. No one told her what to do. "I can do this. I will do this. I don't need anybody's help. Not even yours."

His expression shuttered. "Well, thanks a lot."

She stared at the wedding dress, her heart aching as if she'd lost her best friend. "What do you want me to say?"

"'I'm sorry' would be a good start."

She'd thought he accepted her for who she was, not who he wanted her to be.

"Why?" Pain, raw and jagged, sliced through her. "So you can get in your plane and fly away with no hard feelings? That's what you do best, isn't it? Take off when you don't get what you want?"

"You're way off base. This has nothing to do with me." His hardened gaze, accusatory. "Nothing will ever be perfect enough for you, Serena. I don't know why I've stuck around and tried."

Emotion clogged her throat. Her stomach clenched. She couldn't breathe.

Everything she'd thought about, dreamed about, and planned for was ending. And she felt helpless to stop it.

She'd known what Kane Wiley was like from the very beginning. He'd told her himself. The quintessential Mr. Wrong, but she had pretended he could be her Mr. Right.

Well, he was right about something. It was time to stop pretending.

"Then I guess," she said, her voice trembling, "you'd better go."

* * *

Kane sat in his rented car, his hands on the steering wheel to keep them from shaking. He needed to calm down before driving away.

He took a deep breath, unsure of what had just happened.

"Why? So you can get in your plane and fly away with no hard feelings? That's what you do best, isn't it? Take off when you don't get what you want?"

Serena had it all wrong. This wasn't about him. He hadn't wanted a relationship. He avoided them like bad fuel, but both had found him in Seattle.

Now, he sat in his car, staring at a brightly lit condo. On the outside looking in. That was how Kane usually liked things. Distant, removed, safe. But at this moment, he felt none of those things. Instead, he felt as if someone had yanked his entire life from him. His home, everything he'd wanted, was gone yet again.

That hurt.

And made him feel stupid.

When would he ever learn? Love equaled pain. No two ways about it.

Maybe he shouldn't have pushed her when she was tired and stressed out, but her mood didn't affect the root problem.

Little Miss Perfection wasn't going to change. Super Serena was back and there to stay. She wanted her perfect life, and he didn't fit in. He'd been a fool to think he could or that she would let him.

Kane should have known better.

Next time...

There wouldn't be a next time.

* * *

Heartbroken over what had just happened, Serena sat in the middle of her living room floor, staring at the dress she'd been working on for days. Over a week, actually. Tears filled her eyes, but she blinked them away. She wanted to cry over Kane. She wanted to cry hard, but she still had too much to do.

She focused on the gown. Even with the new fabric, Calista's dress wasn't coming out right. Serena couldn't ignore the truth any longer. Her broken heart splintered more. She would have to start over. This meant she would never be able to make Calista the dress she deserved to wear on the most special day of her life.

Serena cradled her head in her hands.

My fault.

She'd failed. She'd let her friend down in the worst possible way.

Tears stung Serena's eyes, but surrounded by yards of delicate fabrics and lace, she kept them at bay. Not that she had time to use the fabric to make a new dress from scratch now.

What was she going to do? How was she going to tell Calista?

Serena hugged her knees.

All her plans had disintegrated, leaving her nothing to fall back on, nothing to hold on to or reach for. How could everything have gone from perfect to a disaster so quickly?

"You're too busy chasing your vision of perfection to see something right and real in front of you."

Kane's words slammed into Serena. Her shoulders slumped. She had been trying to do her best. What was wrong with wanting a perfect life or a perfect man or a perfect wedding dress?

Perfect wedding dress.

Serena repeated the word. She straightened and stood. Maybe…

She padded her way to the hall closet and opened the door. Hanging there, wrapped in plain muslin, was her almost completed dream wedding gown.

A perfect wedding dress.

For her perfect marriage to the absolutely wrong-for-her Rupert.

She uncovered the gown.

Serena felt no excitement, no joy, no longing the way she had before. Her needing the dress had simply been a dream, a wish that hadn't come true. Chasing a vision—make that a clouded vision—of perfection, most definitely. She sighed.

But Calista's dream was very much alive. Her and Jason's happily ever after still existed. She deserved this gown to start her new life with her husband.

Not perfect. Not for Serena any longer.

But just right for Calista. And right here.

This gown would be the one.

Serena placed the dress on the mannequin. She grabbed her sketch pad, sat on the floor once again, and drew how she wanted the completed dress to look.

Not for her, but for Calista.

Thirty minutes later, Serena was ready to begin the transformation. However much she hated it, Kane was right. She couldn't do this on her own. She needed help to make sure she got this dress finished on time.

"Just remember, next time, we're here for you. We love you."

Serena knew exactly who to call. She wished Kelsey, Elle, and Jane lived closer, but they would understand. Her local friends would also understand and help her. Nothing, not time or tiredness, would stop them from creating a spectacular wedding gown for Calista.

* * *

Oohs and aahs filled the dress design studio on Monday night after Belle had put out the Closed sign and locked the front door. The only question remaining was whether the bride liked the gown or not. Serena held her breath.

"It's absolutely perfect." Tears glistened in Calista's eyes as she stared at her reflection in the three-panel mirror. She spun around on the carpeted platform. "I love it even more than the first dress."

So did Serena. She hadn't let her friend down.

The dress she'd spent weeks designing and stitching with "I do" in mind was no longer hers. Each stitch, each bead, each crystal might have been sewn with love in mind, but not the forever kind. The friend kind.

She'd turned the dress into Calista's dream gown. Sleek and neat, not at all what Serena had planned for herself, but perfect for Calista.

Belle clasped her hands to her chest. "You are the most beautiful bride."

Calista's smile lit up her face. "You say that to all the brides."

"Because it's true."

Calista stared at her reflection in the mirror. "Thank you, Serena."

"Don't thank me." Serena had learned her lesson in time to save Calista's wedding gown but not in time to salvage her relationship with Kane. "We all worked on the dress for the past two days."

"Thank you, everyone." Calista's voice bubbled with excitement.

Everyone spoke at the same time. Laughed. Hugged.

Calista looked at Serena. "Is it horrible if I say I'm glad you got stuck in the wilderness and the other dress got ruined?"

"Not at all," Serena said.

"I know Kane has been a big help to you. I want to thank him." Calista glowed the way only a bride could. "Is he around?"

"I haven't heard from him." The honest answer tore Serena's heart in two. "He might have left Boston."

The studio went dead quiet. Sympathetic eyes focused on Serena.

"I've seen how he looks at you, darlin'." Belle touched her shoulder. "He'll be back."

Serena knew he wasn't coming back. She wanted to apologize after all he'd done for her. For the past two days, she'd tried calling him on his cell phone and at Charlie's. He hadn't returned any of her messages.

"It's okay," she said to her friends. The same as she'd texted and promised on calls from Kelsey, Jane, and Elle. It was okay.

And it was. Or it would be. Someday.

Kane had made his choice, and so had Serena. He didn't want her if she didn't behave the way he wanted, but she was tired of trying to please others all the time. She wouldn't do it any longer. Especially for someone who ran away from commitment, the very thing she wanted most of all.

She couldn't be what he wanted, and he couldn't give her what she wanted. That, unfortunately, was the bottom line.

* * *

"She's a beauty, son," Dad said about the business jet Kane wanted to buy two days later. "But have you thought this through?"

"I'm a pilot. Flying is how I make my living. I need a plane."

"Do you want to go back to that lifestyle, flying here and there, never staying in one place, with one person, for long?"

"I never left that life." Kane stared at the inch-thick sales contract. Grandpa had guaranteed what the insurance payout wouldn't cover and didn't want the amount to be repaid as long as he could be flown places occasionally. The only thing missing? Kane's signature on the paperwork. "I like my freedom."

"You can change how you live and still experience freedom."

Kane thought about Serena, with her wide blue eyes and big, warm smile. He'd been willing to try, but she hadn't been willing to accept the man he'd tried so desperately to be for her. "I don't need to change anything."

"I used to think that way," Dad said quietly. "But after your mother…"

Kane looked up from the contract. "After Mom what?"

Dad stared down at his shoes. "I loved your mother so much. She was my life. After she died, I missed her so much, and I wasn't ready to face what had happened. I wasn't ready to change. I liked being married. I liked having someone there."

"So you married Evangeline."

Dad nodded. "I was looking for a replacement more than anything. I know it hurt you, Kane."

"It did." A ball of emotion clogged his throat. "I

guess I'd been in denial or something, but when you got married, it made Mom's death seem more real. I finally had to accept she wasn't coming back, but I wasn't ready to do that. I couldn't understand how you were ready to do that so quickly."

"Losing your mother was the hardest thing I've ever had to go through. But worse, I lost you, too," Dad admitted. "I hope you can forgive me someday."

Kane didn't want to forgive. Holding on to the grudge—his anger—was easier than opening himself up to more hurt. But he knew that his mother would have wanted him to at least hear his father out. "I'm listening."

"Marrying Evangeline was a mistake. I thought I loved her, but I didn't. I should have listened to you. I should have listened to a lot of people. I'm so very sorry, son." The sincerity in Dad's voice struck a chord deep inside Kane. "I don't know if I'll ever love another woman the way I loved your mother. That doesn't mean I can't love a different way. There is someone I would like to pursue a relationship with if she'll have me, but I want your blessing this time."

"Are you talking about Belle?"

"Yes."

Kane took a deep breath and exhaled slowly. A part of him understood what Dad was talking about. The other part still hurt. But holding on to his anger made little sense. He couldn't change what had happened. Not with Dad. Not with Mom.

"Why Belle?" he asked.

"She understands what it means to lose a spouse. She'll never try to take your mother's place. Belle is independent and driven. We make good partners because we are both set in our ways, ways that complement each other."

It sounded like Dad had put some thought into this. Kane wouldn't stand in his way. "If that's who you care for, go for it, Dad."

"Thank you, son," Dad said, his voice grateful. "What about you and Serena?"

"It's complicated."

"Love always is."

Love?

"I tried to ignore your mother's death and live my life the way I always had. But I learned you must face things head-on, whether or not it's easy. There's no avoiding the bad stuff, even if you think running away is the solution. If you don't do it now, you'll only have to do it later."

His father's words sank in. Had Kane been avoiding whatever went wrong in his life or getting upset when he didn't get his way and holding grudges?

"So you can get in your plane and fly away with no hard feelings? That's what you like to do best, isn't it? Take off when the going gets tough?"

Serena's words replayed in his mind. He thought about his mother's death, his dad's second marriage, Amber's misguided ultimatum, and so many other things, including Serena herself. She was right. He had run away. And he was doing it again.

"No matter what you decide, I love you." Dad patted Kane's shoulder. "I'll always be here for you, son."

And that was what it was all about, Kane realized. Being there for those you cared about. He didn't want to spend his entire life flying from place to place. He remembered the home his parents had created for him, the love inside the walls.

Something so good wasn't easy to make happen. There were no guarantees, and the hard stuff required work. He'd avoided that all these years, but he was finally ready.

He just hoped he wasn't too late.

"Thanks, Dad," Kane said. "I'm sorry it took us so long to talk about this."

Dad smiled. "We have plenty of time ahead of us."

"Just not right now." Kane moistened his dry lips. "Could you give me a lift?"

"Where to?"

"Wherever Serena might be, but we may need to make a stop or two on the way."

"Come on." Dad headed down the stairs of the plane. "You navigate, and I'll drive."

Kane preferred being behind the wheel, but this time, he'd happily sit in the passenger seat. "Let's go."

* * *

Serena cleaned up the mess in her living room, piling the fabric, lace, tulle, and beading into a box. Once this stuff was back at the studio, she could put the entire wedding dress fiasco behind her. Too bad she couldn't do the same with Kane.

Kane.

Tears welled in her eyes. Serena hadn't known him that long, but she'd never experienced such emptiness, such loneliness since he'd been gone. Her heart felt as if all the blood had been squeezed out. Every beat hurt. She picked up the stuffed wolf from the couch.

How had she come to this? All her plans in ashes. Her plans...

Serena nearly laughed. Her plans hadn't been worth much. They hadn't kept her from falling in love with Mr. Wrong. She hugged the wolf.

Her heart still wanted Kane. No one else would do even though he could never give her the kind of love and commitment she wanted. The truth cut deep, the raw wound threatening to swallow her whole. She wiped tears from the corners of her eyes.

Pathetic.

She'd wanted to be loved so badly, to have a family of her own, that she had been willing to engineer her future, plan everything, including the man she wanted to marry. She set the wolf down. At least she'd recognized the trap and wouldn't be caught in it again.

If only...

No. Serena wasn't looking back. She didn't want to

look forward, either. She needed to stop planning and start living.

A knock sounded at her front door.

Serena wasn't expecting anyone. She picked up a tissue and blew her nose.

Another knock.

Go away.

And another.

The doorbell rang.

Fed up, Serena tossed the tissue in the garbage can and stormed to the door. "This had better be important."

She threw open the door and saw...

"Kane."

Tears exploded from her eyes.

"Serena?" he asked, his voice filled with concern.

She must have looked a fright. No makeup, unwashed hair, grungy clothes, and puffy red eyes. "Yes?"

"Seeing you like this..." He wiped the tears from her face with his thumb and led her inside, closing the door behind him. "I'm sorry. I shouldn't have left the way I did. I should have returned your calls, but you're right. Anytime something doesn't go right, I run away. I may think I'm chasing freedom, but all I'm doing is holding on to grudges and not looking back because it hurts too much."

Serena stared at him, shocked yet hopeful. She wiped her eyes, her tears suddenly drying up. She wanted to believe him.

His gaze lingered, practically caressed. "You and I aren't so different, Blondie."

"I'm sorry, too," Serena said, her eyes locked on his. "You were right about me. I get so focused on a goal that I ignore everything else, every other possibility, including what's right in front of my face. Whether it's a wedding dress or…"

Choked up, she couldn't continue.

"We like having control of a situation, but when we don't, it's difficult." Kane inhaled sharply. "When my mother died, I had no control over anything. One minute, I was trying to help my father, and then the next thing I knew, he was dating, engaged, and remarried. I did the only thing I could. I left. I'm tired of leaving, Serena."

Her eyes met his. "But you said that's what you wanted to do. You want freedom—"

"I do, but freedom is no longer enough. I want more."

Serena was almost afraid to ask, but she had to know. "What do you want now?"

"You."

The air whooshed from her lungs. She struggled to breathe, to think.

"But flying is your life," she managed.

He smiled. "My job is flying. Loving you is my life."

Her heart melted. Her knees nearly gave way.

"I don't care if we're in Boston or stranded in the

wilderness, whether you're designing wedding gowns or gathering firewood—I want to be with you. And I mean you, whoever you want to be. Serena, Super Serena, or Blondie."

Serena touched her hand to her heart, which seemed to be dancing to a tune of its own. "I don't know what to say."

"You don't have to say anything." His sincerity brought a lump to her throat. "I love you."

The words she'd wanted to hear. She'd waited to hear them. But she'd had it all wrong. No special plans were necessary to say those words. The words themselves were perfect no matter when or where they were spoken. Even if she looked as if she hadn't slept in days.

She swallowed. Hard. "I love you, too."

Kane pulled her toward him and kissed her. He kissed her lips, her cheeks, her neck. She felt as if he were kissing her heart and her soul. She couldn't have been happier or felt more complete.

"I always had to be the good girl and never disappoint, so I always tried to do the right thing, say the right words, never deviating from my plan. And that worked. Until I met you."

She pulled back and gazed into his eyes.

"I needed to give Calista the chance for the kind of wedding I always wanted, with a dress she'd always remember, but pushing myself to my limit took its toll on my time, my temper, and us. I learned my lesson, though. When I finally realized I couldn't finish the dress myself, I called my friends for help, but by then, you were…"

Gone.

The unspoken word echoed between them.

He ran his finger along her jawline. "I'm here now."

"Yes, you are." A peace filled her. "I finally realized I don't have to be Super Serena all the time. I don't always have to do the right thing. In fact, I've learned I can even be wrong about what's right for me, especially about something very important."

"What's that?"

"Who was Mr. Wrong, and who is Mr. Right."

His smile crinkled the corners of his eyes. "Who might that be?"

She stood on her tiptoes and kissed him hard on the lips.

"You are creative, smart, generous, and beautiful, Blondie." His rich laughter wrapped itself around her heart. "I love you so much."

Joy filled her heart and overflowed. "I love you, too."

"Just to prove I mean what I said…" He dropped down on one knee and pulled something from his pocket. "Will you marry me?"

She stared at the small glass slipper he held with his fingers. Inside was a simple, elegant diamond ring. She knew in her heart this was right. Not only was this the beginning of their fairy tale, but it was the start of a much better life. A life full of love.

"This ring belonged to my mother," he said. "It probably has to be resized. Or if you don't like it, I can buy you another. I want it to be perfect."

Serena put her fingers over his mouth. She didn't need to look at the ring. All she had to see was the love in Kane's eyes, real and right in front of her. "It's already perfect. I love it."

"Does that mean..."

"Yes." Her insides tingled. She had never felt so content or fulfilled in her life. "I love you. I would be honored to marry you, Kane Wiley. Or should I call you Mr. Right?"

"Call me whatever you want." He picked her up and twirled her around. "I don't care as long as we're together."

She laughed. "You know this means I have to design another wedding dress."

He set her down. "I can't wait to see what you come up with for yourself."

Thinking about standing at the altar with Kane beside her, Serena smiled. "Neither can I."

EPILOGUE

The Starr Mountain Lodge, a boutique hotel in Vermont, was the perfect setting for Serena and Kane's wedding. Belle and Kelsey had done the planning, and it was better than Serena could have ever dreamed. Kane seemed pleased too. The elegant and comfortable inn had an inviting fireplace and arched windows with views of snow-covered mountains. It reminded her of their little cabin in that meadow in Idaho.

Not even Serena's parents choosing not to attend the wedding could lessen how wonderful today was. Having Morgan, who had become Belle's personal assistant, and Brayden there was more than enough. And it was Mom and Dad's choice—their loss—for not accepting Kane Wiley as a worthy son-in-law or wanting their daughters and grandson to be a part of their lives.

Serena glanced around the reception. No detail had been overlooked. Guests enjoyed champagne cocktails and passed appetizers while the wedding party had photographs taken. A delicious catered sit-down dinner was served, then followed by Nadia's cake, a four-tiered confection with two layers of chocolate with orange-flavored-fudge filling, her favorite, and two with white chocolate with raspberry filling, Kane's favorite.

Now that the food and cake had been served, guests joined others on the dance floor, moving to the music of a talented DJ. Charlie danced with his arms around Belle. The couple seemed to have gotten closer in the months since the plane crash in Idaho.

The song's lyrics about believing in fairy tales brought a sigh to Serena's lips. She'd found her happy ending with Kane. She leaned back against him, resting against his strong chest as if she'd been doing it her entire life.

He wrapped his arms around her, and his warm breath caressed her neck. "I hope this was the wedding you wanted."

Once upon a time, Serena would have answered differently, but now…now that she'd experienced a love so wonderful, so right, she had no doubt. "It's perfect. Honestly, any kind of wedding would have been perfect as long as we ended up married. That's the most important thing about today."

"I agree."

Serena stared at her hand, at the four-prong-set diamond solitaire engagement ring that had belonged to Kane's late mother. "What matters is how much I love you and what happens after today."

"Have I told you how much I love you?" Kane whispered.

"About ten minutes ago."

"I won't wait so long next time."

Serena smiled as Kane kissed her neck.

Nadia's twins, who'd been their flower girls, ran across the dance floor chased by Brayden, who'd been the ring bearer. The girls looked so sweet and innocent in their white dresses with sage ribbons that Serena designed. Brayden wore a smart-looking tuxedo, though his bowtie had already come off.

"I hope our children look exactly like you," Kane said, his voice full of warmth and love.

Kelsey came closer. "Come on, newlyweds. You have one more thing to do before you leave tonight."

The DJ requested that all single women make their way onto the dance floor.

Serena laced her fingers with Kane's. "I can't wait to see who's next."

"Isn't that an old wives' tale?" Kane asked.

She shrugged, but so far, both she and Kelsey had caught bridal bouquets, and now they were both married. A wedding myth or wedding bliss? Serena would go with the latter.

"You'd better get out there," Kelsey said to someone, and Serena didn't have to turn around to know it was likely Jane and Elle. "Both of you, too."

Elle groaned. "I'd rather catch the flu than the bouquet."

Jane nodded. "Same."

Serena laughed at her friends. Maybe Nadia or Aubrey or Morgan would catch the bouquet instead. Belle would love to plan another wedding for one of them after Calista's wedding at the Castle at Boston University had gone off without a hitch. Serena stood with her back to the crowd and held the bouquet in the air for all to see.

Calista had outdone herself with the flowers, and this tossing bouquet was a smaller version of the one Serena had carried down the aisle. The stems of white dendrobium orchids, green roses, green cymbidium orchids, and white and green parrot tulips were tied with white satin ribbon. Serena wound up her arm as if she were pitching a fastball for the Red Sox and let her bouquet fly. Over the heads of the reaching women and right into the arms of…

Jane.

The smile on Serena's face widened. She glanced at Kane. "This should be interesting."

* * * * *

Thanks for reading *The Dress Designer's Promise.* I hope you enjoyed Serena and Kane's story. If you want to read the next book in the Wedding Bliss series, *The Caterer's Wish,* featuring Jane Dawson, you can find it at melissamcclone.com/wedding-bliss-series.

If you want to know more about Jake Porter and his OMSAR unit in *His Christmas Wish,* you can find it at melissamcclone.com/mountain-rescue-series.

Join my newsletter to receive a FREE story and hear about upcoming and new releases, sales, freebies, and giveaways. Go to melissamcclone.com/subscribe.

I appreciate your help spreading the word. Please tell a friend who loves sweet romance about this book and leave a review on your favorite book site. Reviews help readers find books!

Thanks so much!

About the Author

USA Today bestselling author Melissa McClone has written over sixty sweet contemporary romance and women's fiction novels. She lives in the Pacific Northwest with her husband. She has three young adult children, a spoiled Norwegian Elkhound, and cats who think they rule the house. They do!

If you'd like to find Melissa online:
www.melissamcclone.com
www.facebook.com/melissamcclonebooks
www.facebook.com/groups/McCloneTroopers

OTHER BOOKS BY MELISSA MCCLONE

The Beach Brides/Indigo Bay Miniseries
Prequels to the Berry Lake Cupcake Posse series…

Jenny	*Sweet Do-Over*
Sweet Holiday Wishes	*Sweet Yuletide*
Sweet Beginnings	*Indigo Bay Collection*

The Berry Lake Cupcake Posse Series
Can five friends save their small town's beloved bakery?

Cupcakes & Crumbs	*Kittens & Kisses*
Tiaras & Teacups	*Wishes & Weddings*

Standalone Berry Lake Christmas Book
The Last Cottage on Pinewood Lane

Silver Falls Series
The Andrews siblings find love in a small town in WA state.

The Christmas Window	*A Cup of Autumn*
A Slice of Summer	*A Sprinkle of Spring*

One Night to Forever Series
Can one night change your life, and your relationship status?

Fiancé for the Night	*A Little Bit Engaged*
The Wedding Lullaby	*Love on the Slopes*
The One Night To Forever Box Set	

The Billionaires of Silicon Forest
Who will be the last single man standing?

The Wife Finder	*The Gold Digger*
The Wish Maker	*The Kiss Catcher*
The Deal Breaker	*The Game Changer*

The Bet Makers (Newsletter exclusive)
The Billionaires of Silicon Forest Prequels
The Billionaires of Silicon Forest Series

Mountain Rescue Series
Finding love in Hood Hamlet
with a little help from Christmas magic…

His Christmas Wish	*His Second Chance*
Her Christmas Secret	*His Christmas Family*
Her Christmas Kiss	

Her Royal Duty
Royal romances with charming princes and dreamy castles...

The Accidental Princess	*The Not-So-Proper Princess*
The Reluctant Princess	*The Proper Princess*

Quinn Valley Ranch
Two books featuring siblings in a multi-author series...

Carter's Cowgirl	*Summer Serenade*
Quinn Valley Ranch Two Book Set	

A Keeper at Heart Series
These men know what they want, and love isn't on their list.
But what happens when each meets a keeper?

The Groom	*The Husband*
The Soccer Star	*The Date*
The Boss	*The Tycoon*

For the complete list of books, go to
melissamcclone.com/books

Made in United States
North Haven, CT
12 April 2024

51237076R00150